THE MAGIC TRUCKING COMPANY

Other novels by J.P. Robideaux

The Rick Blaine Series
Escape Into Rain
It's Reigning in London

Boris Thinks I'm Funny

The Magic Trucking Company

A Moving Christmas Story

JP Robideaux

Deep Breath • Spokane, Washington

Dedication

For Jordan, Sarah, Luna and London.

History is the reality of belief, especially at Christmas.
—Paraphrasing Napoleon Bonaparte

Our story takes place, primarily, in the central part of Washington State known to many locals as a crossroads for agricultural commerce, recreation, and, unfortunately, illegal drugs. There are many good reasons to live in any one of the eight counties that make up the center of Washington State, but let's put that part of our story on hold for now, and turn our attention further south — all the way down to the State of Arizona to the border between the United States and Mexico to the dusty Mexican border town of Nogales.

The main streets of Nogales, Mexico, are kept as clean as possible in order to please the tourists and add to the local employment of willing citizens. As the mayor of the northern Mexican city declared recently, "Clean streets require clean sweeps." He went on to explain that merely brushing the surface once, in one direction, is not enough. "Sweep with gusto, back and forth before moving on to pick up your sweepings." Cheers could be heard from a few of the older street sweepers in attendance. They knew how much the elderly mayor liked to be appreciated in his public appearances. Sweepers of all ages managed to live on what they received from street vendors, restaurant owners and the occasional public official in order to provide the daily service. The city provided the brooms and dust bins on wheels, which were, surprisingly, kept in good condition and stored behind a small building that served as the Nogales City Hall in the central part of the city. The Sweepers were also called upon to decorate the downtown area for various festivals such as the Day of the Dead, and Christmas. The downtown main street was decorated all through October to the morning of November 2nd with skulls and skeletons in lighted black and white arrangements that magically turned into the greens and reds of Christmas by November 3rd. Everyone admired the street sweepers of Nogales.

The back alleyways and residences with nearby open sewers and trash heaps were another matter and never a priority. How the people of Nogales lived did not interfere with their ability to earn a living. Smiles and friendly attitudes were known to come more easily to the youngsters who participate in begging, as everyone is encouraged to welcome the visiting public who can't wait to spend.

Residents of the small city tread on the daily exercise wheel of thankfulness for the mostly American dollars that flow south over the border each year. But for Enrique Mara, a 25-year-old street vendor, the challenge of having to smile and out-sell the other vendors felt more and more like a burden. He was tired of humbling himself for the crowds by over emphasizing his accent in order to impress the foreign visitors, mostly old people who couldn't control their bladders let alone their wallets. Smiling, flirting, and cheating had become a way of life for most of the vendors Enrique hung out with after work. If *putting on a good show* were a contest, Enrique would win hands down. It wasn't that the handsome young man meant to be cocky, although he had been accused of it, no, Enrique Mara had a great deal of pride he'd bestowed upon himself. He had no way of knowing anything about himself, until one night.

It happened last year on Christmas Eve. A woman approached his stand of scented candles, bracelets, and necklaces. A shawl covered her head, but Enrique saw beyond the expensive multi-colored linen that covered her face. A strange feeling came over him. He could tell she was an attractive woman, starting with her painted nails, lips and jawline. "May I help you find the perfect gift?" He made the offer as his head lowered with a most inquisitive smile. The woman hesitated and didn't look up at him right away. Instead, she stepped back, removed the shawl from her head and began looking him up and down as if analyzing his appearance. Enrique became nervous, which was not his nature. All he could think of doing in the moment was to restate his question. His voice did not sound familiar to him. Was this woman about to put a spell on him? Once he finished speaking, she stepped forward and in a whispery low voice said, "You are my sister's son. I knew it." Enrique listened as if spellbound as the woman, who stood nearly eye-to-eye with him, went on to say that his mother, Ana, was her only sibling. She added, "I've been looking for you to let you know you have relatives…and…that your mother has, unfortunately, passed. She died of pneumonia two weeks ago. But it was the drugs that really took her life." They stood like statues looking at one another without another word being said. Finally, Enrique came out of his frozen state long enough to shut down his stand, at her request, and go with her to a restaurant around the corner. She brought a hand out of her coat pocket and held it out for him to take and he took it. Her hand felt warm and comforting like the conversation they were about to have. For the next hour she provided Enrique with a photo of his mother, some money, and his real last name. "You have your mother's eyes, Enrique Hernando Valesquez, and you should be proud my nephew. You come from good people." She reached out over the table and held him by his shoulders and looked him straight in his bright blue eyes. He knew he should feel grateful and tried to smile.

Enrique suddenly felt nauseous and nearly walked away from the lady and the shrimp tacos he'd eaten. Filled with more confusion and questions than shrimp, Enrique smiled at the woman, pushed his chair back and excused himself as he headed for the restroom. He splashed water in his face and looked closely into the mirror above the sink. "My mother's eyes?" He suppressed the anger beginning to well up inside of him by pounding the sink and drying his hands over and over again.

When he returned to the table the woman calling herself his aunt had paid the bill and was gone. The restaurant owner said she was wiping tears as she left. Enrique thanked the owner, and heard the lock click as he returned to his stand. He sat down slowly on the old wooden stool in a daze for a few minutes watching the thinning holiday crowd pass. He forced himself to move and decided not to open for evening business. Hurriedly, Enrique rushed through the motions of closing his stand, including the gifting of a large scented candle to a customer who couldn't decide. "Felice Navidad." A few minutes later he left for his small apartment. Still in a daze, he rushed along the street before turning into a dark alley, two blocks from where he lived. A cat made way as Enrique splashed through a series of puddles before heading up the stone back staircase leading to the red outer door of his sanctuary. Once inside, he placed the photo of his mother on the kitchen table next to the $300 in American bills that had been handed to him by Ana, his mother's sister. Ana, the mysterious dark-haired beauty. He suddenly stood and grabbed the back of his chair, lifting it up over the table. He was furious. Shaking. He felt like throwing it against the wall.

Instead, he sat heavily and wept until he ran out of tears. By the time he dried his face in the small bathroom, Enrique made another decision that night. He would keep the last name he'd invented — Mara, taken from a former Hispanic hero. That decision, made when he was much younger, allowed him to feel the pride the government lady, whose first name he didn't know, had mentioned. For the time being he would rely on the family he had depended on up to this point — a kind relief worker and the friends he made at the orphanage. They were his people from the time he was left alone on a street corner at the age of five. That corner was a distant memory, but much like the corner where he transacted business daily in Nogales. Enrique ran with a group of boys that had his back, learning to survive together. Survival became his teacher, fed him when he was hungry and covered him up at night when it was cold.

Enrique and his trusted amigos would share stories of how easily they were able to sell inferior merchandise, some made in China, for high prices. But the best scams came at night after the tourists had been drinking and let their guard down, especially the people from the cooler climates up north in the U.S.A. Enrique revealed a different persona at night – a change that even caught his friends off guard at times. For the last few years, Enrique discovered how much he enjoyed being bad under the cloak of darkness. The adrenaline rush gave him a new feeling of success and power. The planning and participation in selling drugs led to making more money and developing new relationships. He knew he had to be careful, but so far everyone involved stayed true to their word.

Mexican nights in the late summer encourage tourists to relax and enjoy and forget all their worries. Whether it's watching an oblique sun set on the ocean or a sunrise over a lush championship golf course, there were plenty of vistas to please every taste. And Enrique enjoyed helping them by selling trinkets and gadgets in the daytime mixed with a variety of illegal drugs, on the side, at night. Adults of all ages came back to Enrique's stand more than once, mostly young women who secretly called him a "Charmer" behind his back. It could have been his black curly hair, blue eyes, or the fact that Enrique worked-out, sometimes attacking a pull-up bar in the back of his stand with his six foot-two inch frame in a sweaty sleeveless tank top shirt. He had a growing list of return customers, which also pleased his handlers. An attractive young lady once asked him for his name. She wanted to know more about the handsome young man handing her change. He told her a story he'd invented in case the subject came up. As he told her about being named after his grandfather and that the family name was connected to a mythological character, she came around the stand. "Let's find a quiet place where no one cares who we are or what we're doing." Enrique immediately closed the stand a half hour early and left with the woman.

The men managing the street vendors didn't care to know Enrique's history. All they paid careful attention to was his ability to sell. And could Enrique sell. If they had an item that others found hard to sell they'd give it to Enrique. A few months ago his skills were tested with 500 plaster owls that stood about a foot high — colored in various browns and blacks with yellow eyes. Instantly, Enrique came up with an idea. Instead of placing the statuettes out in front of his stand in large groups, he kept only two at a time on the back of his stand under a sign that read: Relics from a Mayan Cave. Within a week the 500 were gone, and at higher than expected prices. That accomplishment, among others, were written up in notes passed on to the cartel who carefully supervised the retail operations in Nogales under their control.

One night after spending the entire day in the hot sun, Enrique closed up his stand and headed for his apartment a mile away. As he turned the corner off the main street into a back alley, three men dressed in black came up to him. Enrique had already made the cash drop with his supplier and let the men know. "We're not here for money, Enrique, you are to be the guest, tonight, of Senior Morales. Enrique nearly fell over when he heard the name. The taller of the three asked if he was all right. Enrique nodded his head. Senior Morales was a very popular official in the Nogales community. He had the reputation as a benevolent leader, working to feed the hungry and provide services to the needy. There were also suspicions that he had connections to the cartels. Enrique knew more about the suspicions than the man's philanthropy. He took a minute as the taller man looked at a watch. Enrique thought it was odd that Morales wanted to meet with a street vendor. *Why me? Why now?*

Chapter 1

The old Ford fought the driver for control as the truck rounded exit 110 from I-90 heading south toward Yakima and his last stop of the day. Each of the company's drivers had a special name for the truck with nearly four hundred thousand miles on the odometer — Old Reliable was used the most. Even though Chet was a son of the company's founder, Bruce (Pops) Bellman, the young rookie became the driver of choice for the old Ford, especially at busy times like today. Chet didn't mind, he loved the job, especially navigating along new territory on long out-of-town routes. The earlier deliveries to retail stores in Moses Lake ran smoothly all morning. It wasn't until his afternoon deliveries to outlying farms and ranches that he, literally, ran into trouble. He'll admit that he was checking his map and trying to drive at the same time when it happened. Chet looked up in time to see antlers passing in front of the truck. Moments later, Chet had to break hard for the rest of the family, a doe and her fawn. The incident happened a few miles back and he was still shaking. The deer, unhurt, ran off, but Chet noticed a steering problem right away. He hoped the last load in the back hadn't come untethered. He would check it as soon as he found a spot to pull over.

He was on his own today and being the youngest in his family trucking business, Chet felt he had more to prove than his two older brothers. One thing he knew for sure, the front-end alignment on the truck would have to be checked, which, as he thought about it, might be one of many fixes the old rolling workhorse needed. But that wasn't up to Chet as he carefully maneuvered around a pothole the size of an average wash basin.

Chet Bellman could clearly hear his father cussing out the county road crew for overlooking a deep hole in the road's surface as if he'd been sitting next to him today. As a youngster barely able to sit on the seat of the truck with his feet touching the floorboard, he'd often hear his father say, *Son, cover your ears.* Chet did plenty of *ride-alongs* with his dad when he was younger. One evening after arriving home with his Pops, Chet dropped his fork and said a swear word in front of his mother at the dinner table, causing his father to dive further into his gravy and potatoes. Without skipping a beat, his mother, who sat at the other end of the table, dabbed the corner of her mouth, replaced her napkin, then turned to look at each of Chet's four siblings, who were doing their best not to laugh or choke. She then gently turned her gaze on Chet and asked where he'd heard *that* word. The youngster put down his utensil, wiped his mouth with his napkin, glanced quickly at his father, who was no help, which didn't go unnoticed by mom. "I'd like to talk to you both after dinner," she said in a lady-like whisper. "Mellissa, would you please pass your father more potatoes and gravy. He seems to be very hungry all of a sudden." There was a noticeable amount of redness in Chet's face and a definite difference in Pops's vocabulary around his youngest, in the truck, after that dinner-time slip.

Chet laughed out loud and patted the dashboard at the memory of his time with Pops as he watched for more potholes along the unfamiliar stretch of asphalt. Maintenance of the trucks and anything mechanical, at the Magic Trucking Company, had to be reported to Pops first. He had a way of keeping the three older trucks running in spite of his sons' urgings to replace them. Chet made a mental note to tell his father about his challenging day of driving as he headed for his last delivery in record-setting heat of 101 degrees. At least the air conditioning on the old beast worked. And, as if on cue, just as he finished that thought, a clicking sound, similar to putting a playing card in bicycle spokes, began to build in one of the cooling vents. "Aw, come on! Not now," Chet bellowed as his fist hit the dashboard once and then harder a second time, just above the vent. *Problem solved.* One more mental note to make. He enjoyed long drives, especially if the A/C worked on hot sunny days like today.

Driving into a blue sky all day gave Chet time to think about his future, and the options he and his father had recently reviewed. Pops urged his youngest son to consider a career in the family business of freight delivery, residential and commercial moving, and storage. "There's a bright future for you here, son," his father offered with a smile. Chet knew his father was worried about the future of The Magic Trucking Company, since Pops faced some lingering health challenges, having just celebrated his 70th birthday. Chet told his father that he would seriously consider staying, and wanted to take the summer before making a final decision. Chet also enjoyed the outdoors, so his other option was to become a professional outfitter, leading clients throughout the northwest. The outdoors was a lifestyle that the whole Bellman family enjoyed together, hunting, fishing and camping. A lifestyle that had been handed down over four generations of Bellmans in Washington State.

The truck, fortunately, became much easier to control on smooth straight driving asphalt as he carefully maneuvered through the Yakima Valley countryside. He increased his speed up to the truck limit of 65 mph after stopping at a scenic outlook to check the load and take in the view. The stop helped confirm that the load was fine, and it also helped Chet to chill by pouring water over his head after taking several sips, as he worked through the heat of the day. Winding down evidently involved switching to one hand on the wheel, an automatic reflex that put a smile on his face. Chet and Old Reliable were flying along in sync. He scanned the whole road as he drove, checking the shoulders and the horizon more than ever, partially because of the near deer accident. But mostly due to his father's driver training, which began when he was 10. He'd just gotten used to the smooth road surface…and then he noticed it, not far up ahead, the dark color of pavement disappeared as the fence line continued. "Damn!" Chet took his earbuds out, placed them in his shirt pocket, and prepared for the pull to the left in steering that would undoubtedly occur with the change in road surface from asphalt to gravel on dirt.

Sure enough, the asphalt gave way to gravel like an uncomfortable baton exchange in track competition, and within a quarter mile, a large, swirling, tan colored cloud began to build behind the old Ford as the now familiar tugging pull in the steering began to challenge him.

Chet knew most of the addresses along the Yakima River, but he'd never been in this part of the county. Even though he liked the countryside, unfamiliar territory made the work day last longer than he planned. Chet decided that the heat and the additional time today were not going to get him down. He would make this last stop his best on his schedule. The day may appear to be ending on a hot and dusty note, but not his attitude. He couldn't wait to return with an empty truck and a stack of signed bills of lading. He will beat his own personal daily delivery record, 16, by one, with this one last delivery. And, like *magic*, he'd be hauling his tired body and his hard-working old truck 100 miles back to Moses Lake. Chet smiled to himself with the thought, which was reflected on a bumper sticker that adorned the back side of all the MTC vehicles. The sticker read: *Like Magic, I'm headed back to Moses Lake.* Chet's mom came up with the saying years ago. She said it was how she felt about Pops, driving all over Central Washington delivering every type and size of item in all kinds of weather. She didn't know how he did it sometimes, but just like a magician, he made those deliveries happen like David Copperfield in his Las Vegas show. "One moment the trucks are full, the next everything is gone. Whoosh!"

Chet hoped to check in before six o'clock when Pops normally left the office for home. He not only had to tell Pops about the steering and fan problems on the truck, Chet wanted to ask his dad for a few days off to go fishing with his buddies along the Columbia River. The wide running channel of fresh water ran along the southern border of the State of Washington and hosted some of the most challenging fishing in the continental U.S. This trip would be devoted to the summer run of salmon-like trout known as Steelhead.

As the youngest in the family of three brothers and two sisters, Chet found it easier to ask and be granted favors. At twenty years of age, he liked to think that one day, if he chose to stay, he could earn a management position in the family trucking operation. But, being the youngest, he knew he had to prove himself first.

Chet quickly switched his thoughts from favors to work while checking his location. The GPS on his phone showed his destination coming up, about a mile away. He had to resort to Google Maps because the area had very few road signs. Finally, off in the distance, a large dark-colored gate came into view. The white lettering really stood out under a huge, gold colored horseshoe, hanging over the name: *Hawthorne Ranch.* He wondered why he hadn't seen this part of the county before. He felt as though the ranch had popped up out of nowhere. The further he drove the more he became amazed — this place went on forever. He could tell because of the unique style of white fencing featuring black letters H/R that could be seen every quarter mile.

He slowed the truck as the gate entrance came closer and pulled hard to the right in order to make the turn in time to rumble over the cattle guard. It took all the strength he had, fighting the steering problem. He looked forward to parking Old Reliable and walking away at the end of the day. The large metal grates were placed in the roadbed, on both sides of the gate, preventing cattle from escaping when the gate was open. They were the largest metal gates Chet had ever seen. *How big is this place?*

He angled the truck close to a bronze and black call box with a number display and pushed the code, which was on the delivery manifest. The black iron gate made a low growling sound as it slowly separated, sending two equal partitions backward like the mouth of a giant monster opening wide then wider. Chet went from glaring at the gate to looking at the speaker as a deep-throated male voice instructed him to proceed slowly forward. He put the truck in gear with a slight grinding sound and proceeded across the grates and onto a smooth black asphalt surface. As soon as the tires hit the asphalt, a Welcome sign with a posted 15 mph speed limit greeted him.

The surface of the driveway reminded Chet of a dark black snake as the asphalt serpentined around some large boulders through a row of twenty-foot Ponderosa pine trees that lined the roadway for another quarter mile. The trees were perfectly trimmed with branches starting six feet up the trunk of each tree from the roadbed. Chet adjusted his aviators as he watched a herd of Hereford and Angus cattle graze in a large field to his left. To his right a herd of horses ran in two nearby pastures. *Busy place — watch the speedometer.* A sleek black stallion broke loose from the pack and raced past his truck as if trying to beat the big van to a large red barn that eventually revealed itself up ahead. The pines disappeared as did the asphalt. Straight ahead stood the barn surrounded by crushed gravel, and to his left the roadway turned off and merged with bronze and gold-colored flagstones set into mortared gravel leading to a large courtyard of the same.

Chet took a deep breath and let it out as an enormous stone-encrusted home with a slate roof, built in a horseshoe shape, appeared to be tossing itself toward the barn. He kept the truck on the gravel as he headed toward the barn. The further he drove the more the place reminded him of European homesteads he'd seen in brochures or on television. Out of the corner of his eye he saw movement. A young lady came out the front door of the ranch house and stood on the porch, waving a leather-gloved hand for him to stop. She pointed to a spot about half way between the house and the barn. Chet rolled down the window as she approached the truck.

"Thought you weren't going to make it, but here you are, just like Magic!" Chet smiled and nodded his head. She slowly walked his way, putting on the second glove. She looked to be about his age. The closer she came the more she resembled a cowhand with mud streaks on her face, dusty boots, jeans and a straw-colored western hat with a thin woven black band that held a gold-colored H/R broach in place in the front. She looked ready to bust another bronc. He'd thought he heard it all when it came to people yelling out the name of their trucking operation, but he liked the way she said the word; *may-gic*. She added a little twang to it that made the word feel different. Chet found himself lost in thought, and for a moment, like he'd wandered into a different world.

Pops came up with the name Magic when he started the business more than thirty years ago in Moses Lake. He'd felt like there needed to be a better delivery service than the ones that came from the bigger cities in the Pacific Northwest, places like Spokane to the east and Seattle to the west, and Portland, Oregon to the south. Pops started with an old farm truck that he bought at auction for more money than it was worth. It took him about two weeks to get the old Chevy into running condition, but when he did he said it was like: Magic! And the name stuck.

The cowhand with dirt on her face made her way closer to the truck. She stood with her hands on her hips and a look on her face as though it was Chet's turn to speak. He stuck his head out the driver's window and gestured with his fingers.

"I just snapped my fingers and found ya. Ah, where do you want the load, Miss?"

"It's not Miss, delivery guy." Chet's heart sank as he waited there looking at her as if he'd been given the worst news possible. " It's Missy, Missy Hawthorne," she said with a big toothy smile. Time stopped, everything went into slow motion. Missy walked ahead of the truck, pointing toward the barn. Chet saw her lips move, but all he heard was the mooing of cattle and the engine of his truck. *What just happened?*

After Chet backed up to the spot where Missy stood, he slipped on his tan colored leather work gloves and hopped out of the truck. At six foot two, and two hundred pounds, with blond hair tied into a ponytail, Chet made an impression on people, especially the ladies, whether he knew it or not. He tried not to get too close, standing back, checking his delivery sheet through dust-covered aviators, sweating in a white crew neck t-shirt, and blue jeans that fit tight over his work boots and around his slim waist. He moved the sunglasses up on his head as he spoke, revealing deep blue eyes.

"Looks like we have twelve cases of Christmas lights, two saddles and some bridles and tack." Chet looked down at the manifest as he continued to read, if he had glanced up just then he would have noticed Missy continuing to smile at him as he spoke. She was a year younger and the youngest of three, two brothers, one deceased, and the other, Tim, who also helped to run the ranch for her father, Jake.

"Yep. You can stack everything over there, next to the pig." Missy pointed to a covered porch that ran the entire length of the barn. "That's Barney. Don't pay him no mind, he'll move quick enough."

There was something about the sound of Missy's voice that made Chet feel very comfortable. Coupling that with her *in your face* attitude and her side of the conversation became more than a little distracting. He'd never encountered anyone like Missy Hawthorne and suddenly found it hard to concentrate on what she was saying. She asked him a few questions about his job as he carried the saddles toward the porch.

"Oh ah, do you mind taking those saddles a little further — into the tack room over there?" Missy pointed straight ahead at a wooden half-door with the word TACK written across the top of the door frame. Further down the loading dock was a bigger sliding barn door. Chet smiled, nodded, and took a deep breath as he picked up the saddles, one in each hand, and kept going. The load was heavy, but Missy could see by his muscular build, the guy had no problem complying with her request as he placed each saddle carefully on the loading dock. She watched as he stacked the entire delivery next to the saddles. They traded looks as Chet waited for further instruction hands on hips. Missy broke the silence, "Sorry, just taking a breath…I mean a break. Follow me." He stepped aside as she brushed past, leading the way up concrete steps to the top of the loading dock.

Missy slid a barn door open revealing a well-organized shop area with a heavy leather smell, in addition to a few other odors associated with barns. Missy noticed the look on Chet's face and could tell right away that this good-looking hunk was impressed by the ranch's tack facility. She pointed straight ahead as she spoke, "You can set the saddles on the floor over there by the work bench." Missy had plenty of things to do, but decided to give him a quick tour of the room that she personally supervised, pointing out details that seemed to amaze him as she checked out his tight fitting jeans that led to his dusty work boots. Chet held the door for Missy as she walked under the bridge of his arm, smiling up as she exited. The tour ended up outside where the boxes of lights were stacked on the dock.

Chet made some comment about it being a little early for Christmas lights. Missy responded by explaining that the lights were going to be strung on the pine trees lining the drive. "We begin stringing lights around the ranch by mid-September not long after Labor Day. 20 to 25 foot trees take a while and we have other things to do as you can see. But we have to begin sometime, right?" Chet nodded as they walked back down the ramp together. He kept going to the back of the truck and pulled down the sliding tailgate rear door, turned the latch and locked it. When he turned around, there she was, standing close enough to be his shadow. "Missy. I ah, need you to sign for the delivery. They both looked at one another and after Missy signed, she shoved the pen in Chet's front pocket of his jeans. "Keep the pen handy, Chet, we'll probably be seeing you next week."

She explained that they had another delivery scheduled. "More Christmas decorations. We're really going all out this year." Chet looked directly into the most beautiful almond-shaped brown eyes and immediately went blank. He knew it was his turn to speak. They both stood there looking at one another. Finally, Chet managed to move his lips. "I'll look forward to seeing you, I...I mean, delivering you — to you is what I'm trying to say." Chet felt an unexpected attack of *Stupid* but moved, somehow, toward the truck and climbed into the driver's seat and started the truck engine. Obviously, he'd become more than a little flustered, a new experience for a guy who never had a problem dating. Besides, he found work, fishing, and hanging with his buddies satisfying enough — at least up until now. Driving off back down the serpentine drive he looked in the rearview mirror and saw her petting Barney the pig as she watched him go. He also saw his own reflection — he was blushing. *Damn.*

Chet kept his speed down as the truck approached an opening gate. A dark-haired man came out from behind one of the pine trees as the truck slowed, waiting for the gate to completely open. "Hey, driver. Stop for a second." The fellow was neatly dressed in black boots and jeans, a red long-sleeved western shirt and sporting a gold-chain necklace with the now familiar H/R logo. He stubbed out a cigarette as he came closer to the truck. Chet had the window down as the man introduced himself. "I'm Tim Hawthorne and you need to know something." Chet could tell the guy had been drinking. "You…you need to make your deliveries *faster.* You took way too long today and that's not… acceptable." Chet had to turn his head away from the breath, but listened politely and when the guy was done, apologized for the delay, put the truck in gear and drove off. As Chet made the turn out the gate, he noticed the man get into an ATV side-by-side and drive off along a dirt path toward the cattle. *Nice to meet you, Tim.*

§

Peter Bellman pushed his sunglasses back up his nose and made a large check mark on the clipboard he carried as Chet drove into the lot. It had become obvious to Peter that his younger brother enjoyed the work and caught on quickly when it came to learning new rules and regulations. Peter felt proud of the kid he used to babysit. Peter swung the heavy cyclone gate shut, flipped the latch and locked it with a heavy chain, now that Chet made it back. He'd radioed Peter earlier to let him know he'd be late. Peter's dark glasses got a good workout as he shook his head in disbelief when the old Ford made its way through the gate and directly into the maintenance area. Noises coming from the old box truck once again, sounded more like money down the drain to Peter. A decision whether to keep and repair or sell had to be done about the last of the old relics. Peter made a note on the clipboard to talk to Pops about the truck as he walked. He had to hurry. The time on Peter's watch read a quarter after six and he needed to leave to meet his wife at their son's soccer match. It was the last game of the summer before school started and Peter made a promise to be there for the match.

"Sorry to keep you waiting, Pete. The last delivery in Yakima took longer than I expected. Oh, and don't forget, Pops needs to check the steering on the truck. The alignment is off, it pulls to the right."

Chet's brother, Peter, the second oldest in the family, had his head down making notes as he and Chet walked across the truck yard. The older brother put his arm around his younger sibling and pulled him close. The two of them had a special bond that grew over time as Pops built his company. Their older brother, Michael, worked part-time at MTC, but the natural athlete had his sights set on college and a possible scholarship. But when that didn't work out he changed his mind and joined the Marine Corps. and ended up in Afghanistan. Pops understood Michael's need to get away and promoted Peter, who took Michael's place and became mentor and guardian to his younger siblings, especially the youngest, Chet.

Peter, the second person in his family to earn a college degree, managed Magic Trucking since their father, Bruce, semi-retired earlier in the year. The old man, having entered his seventh decade, threw his back out for the last time and after a medical check-up, was told to slow down. The matriarch of the family, Margaret Mary Bellman, Maggie to her family and friends, put her foot down and wouldn't allow her Bruce, lovingly referred to as Pops, to leave the house until he promised to retire. The announcement of Pops's retirement was made the following Sunday during their regular family dinner at the Bellman's homestead on the shores of Moses Lake. "Yep, there she was all five foot two inches of her, shaking her finger in my face. I tell ya, I was shaking too, trying not to laugh." The thought of six foot — three inch Pops being given the ultimatum by his much shorter wife made the whole table burst with laughter. "I told your father that it was time he start thinking about himself and learn to relax a little, that's all, what's so funny about that?" She said with a bright smile that warmed the entire room.

Maggie had a sweetness about her that was reflected in their girls, Mellissa and Cindy, who enjoyed watching their mother cleverly explain her actions. Chet sat between his older sisters, Peter sat with his wife, Lois, and their son, Jack. Maggie sat at the opposite end of the table from Bruce — the power end as he liked to call it. There was a ninth place setting for the oldest son, Michael, who was notoriously late for dinner. "Michael is on his way. He said to go ahead." After her announcement, Maggie and Bruce traded looks as Mellissa and Cindy brought the pork roast and salad to the table.

After the meal, Bruce sat at his end of the table with a heating pad comforting his posture. It went without saying that Pops was in charge of the family as long as Maggie approved of his behavior. Family and friends all knew who really ran the household. That went for Pops too. He didn't mind if Maggie, on occasion, would step in and *clarify* something that he'd just declared. But given the opportunity, Pops loved throwing a verbal curveball Maggie's way once in a while, as he did when he retold Maggie's finger-waving ultimatum. After all, the conversation eventually led to his decision to finally retire. He made the incident sound as if he had been held prisoner in his own home, which made for more laughter, as he kept embellishing. Eventually, the discussion turned more serious and they settled on semi-retirement, so long as Bruce kept his *promise*. The promise included reduced hours, home for dinner every night, and no late night or weekend favors for friends that involved a truck and free labor. Instead, Bruce would depend on Peter, Chet, and Michael, to be the muscle and to do favors when required. There were ten years between Peter and Chet, but they worked well together. Michael, the oldest, was another story.

After deploying to Afghanistan for the second time, Marine Sergeant Michael Bellman was wounded by an IED, Improvised Explosive Device, while riding in an armored personnel carrier. As a result, the former athlete lost his left leg from the knee down, and recently developed bouts of Post Traumatic Stress Disorder. After three months of rehab at Walter Reed back east, Michael returned home to his loving family with no idea of what came next for him in life. The family trucking business would always be an option, he knew that. But Michael was never interested in the business, that's why he joined the military service believing that it would provide him with a resume that would land him a job in law enforcement. But soon after his arrival home, Bruce and Maggie, and the rest of the Bellman family, noticed a change in Michael's normally positive attitude and enthusiasm for life. He had gone from being the older brother that everyone, including friends, idolized, to become a quiet, lethargic person they didn't even recognize. The hardest part in welcoming home a wounded war hero was watching them try to transition back into some semblance of what they had been, especially a hard-charging charismatic go-getter like Michael. And to make matters worse, he had to learn to walk all over again.

§

From the first grade on, blonde-haired, blue eyed, Mellissa Bellman loved going to school. There were few experiences in life that thrilled her more than learning new things and being with friends who shared her joy. She would sit wherever the teacher wanted, and preferred the very middle section of the room, surrounded by kids her age. Mellissa couldn't help but smile when she entered the classroom and greeted her teacher. The exception to that feeling came when she was running late or when her regular teacher was sick and she had to deal with a variety of strangers who acted less interested in education and more in general conversation.

Mellissa had expectations, first for herself and, second of those around her. For example, she preferred to be on time for class or any event related to school. In all her years of elementary, high school, and college, she missed only one full day of class, and that was in high school when a student complied with a dare and set off the fire alarm. Mellissa was so upset when she found out it was a friend who hadn't done his homework that caused the daring event. Mellissa disliked being surprised. She expected everything to happen according to what she'd been told.

One time when the flu was going around, her fourth grade teacher, Ms.Ogletree, a favorite of every student in the class, caught the virus and was gone for what seemed a lifetime. As a result, her substitutes, all former teachers, never measured up to the young, outgoing Ms. Ogletree, beginning with a retired older gentleman who could hardly hear and spoke in a low mumble. Thank goodness he only lasted one day, a Friday, but for the next few weeks it was one new teacher after another.

Mellissa's hopes of ever seeing Ms. Ogletree caused her to come up with one of her best ideas ever. Mellissa, along with a few classmates, organized a *Get Well Greeting Card* art project. Mellissa and two of her best friends designed a card that fit into a nine by twelve inch envelope. The cover had hearts and flowers in the shapes of letters that spelled out; Get Well Soon. Most of the students signed their names, a few left a sentiment. Mellissa was the last to sign. Her sentiment read; *Please come back as soon as possible, we miss you so much and we can't take it anymore.* Ms. Ogletree returned the following Monday to a room full of cheers with Mellissa jumping for joy as she wiped away a few tears. As the children gathered around their favorite teacher, a wink from Ms. Ogletree signaled to Mellissa that her idea to create a card was, in fact, her best idea ever.

Maggie and Pops always looked forward to Parent/Teacher nights. The proud parents ran out of responses to compliments about their Mellissa, which just kept coming as they walked the halls of her school. Praise for her positive attitude and friendliness came not just from teachers, but other parents as well, resulting in a great deal of pride for them both.

Mellisa's mother kept a scrapbook for each of her children. They were filled with academic as well as athletic accomplishments. Mellissa had more pages in her book than any of the other four siblings. One of the more treasured additions to the book came from Ms. Ogletree who hand delivered a card of congratulations at Mellissa's college graduation reception. She gave Mellissa a hug and before breaking away whispered in her ear, "I miss seeing you in class."

Even though Mellissa's life appeared to be on cruise control, her mother knew how hard she worked to take and keep control of her life. She helped at home, received good grades in school, developed loyal friendships and volunteered at their church. But there was one thing about their third child that puzzled her parents — Mellissa's passion for the weather and meteorology. "I never understood why a sudden hail storm, when she was only seven years old, captivated her so much," her mother would share with anyone willing to listen. It had been nearly fifteen years since Mellissa and her sister came running into the house when the unexpected storm hit. The noise coming from the fiberglass patio covering made it hard to hear, causing the girls to shout in their excitement. "Mom, what's happening?" Maggie spent the next few minutes holding both girls tight until the storm passed. Cindy, fourth in line, continued to be upset after the noise subsided, but Mellissa appeared to have a sudden sense of wonder over the event that had just occurred. She asked her mother one question after another, each one becoming harder to answer, leaving Maggie with only one recourse, to smother her daughter with a big hug in order to stop her. Mellissa wanted to know all about what caused the hail and why it came with such force. Maggie knew her daughter wouldn't stop asking questions until she had answers, so Maggie came up with an idea.

The next day, Pops and Maggie took both girls to the local weather station for a quick tour — and hopefully some answers. Pops knew the manager, Sonny, who more than welcomed their interest, especially from the little girl with the big smile and pigtails. That visit became Mellissa's favorite memory. She would later call it a *turning point in her life.*

It had been nearly three years since her university graduation, and as she had planned, Mellissa Bellman, journeyman weather forecaster, sat at her computer in the Moses Lake National Weather Service Station. She'd graduated with honors in meteorology and minored in communications. One of her greatest qualities, according to the station manager Sonny

Stellacono, was Mellissa's ability to translate what had been forecasted into more understandable language.

Mellissa smiled as she took a sip of her sugar-free 20 ounce oat milk latte and checked the daily electronic weather maps that dotted the front of the room. She'd just completed her Area Forecast Discussion that would be checked by her Lead Forecaster, Bridgett Hansen, before being released to the media. Bridgett and her husband, Ernesto, had just moved to the Moses Lake area from California. He had a job opportunity in the area and they both wanted to live in the Pacific Northwest. Bridgett, ten years older than Mellissa, transferred from a station in northern California and became the perfect mentor for the younger journeyman.

The Moses Lake station officially became part of the National Weather Service in 1990, an agency of the United States federal government. They were tasked with providing weather forecasts, warnings of hazardous weather, and other related services that affected the safety of the working, traveling, and vacationing public. The Moses Lake station works with other stations in the Pacific Northwest Region starting with Spokane to the east, Pendelton, Oregon to the south, and Seattle to the west. Moses Lake, the smallest station with only ten employees and one station manager, falls in the center of the region and traditionally passes on weather information that is generated from the larger market areas. The Canadian border is less than a hundred air miles to the north, so the northern exposure of weather forecasting fell to the Moses Lake operation. Because all weather stations in the United States are governed by federal authority, the outer doors to the facility were locked with access granted by appointment only.

Moses Lake's identification for all communication is listed as WSML. All internet, phone, two-way radio or mail correspondence referred to those four letters that were emblazoned on a neon-lit sign on the front of the concrete block building. The letters could easily be seen by travelers passing by on I-90 nearly two miles away.

Mellissa's duties would often extend beyond a normal forty-hour work week, but she didn't mind. She loved studying, analyzing and helping to predict weather. She had to be reminded that they were in the business of forecasting, not predicting, the weather. An older colleague explained that forecasting is more like *estimating* what was going to happen, rather than providing a more definite prediction. Mellissa's smile would form and she would nod and use the term *forecast*, but in her mind she wanted to be known for more accurate and concise predictions.

Her normal shift ran from six in the morning to two in the afternoon. But Mellissa would often remain on-site at the weather station for an hour or longer, to help out and gain more knowledge through experience. There was so much more involved with her job than what she'd learned in school. School never taught her how to deal with people. *Who knew?*

Sonny Stellacono literally built the Moses Lake weather station from the ground up. The government provided the funding for the building design and footprint layout, but the short, bald, cigar smoking, Italian had plenty to say about where the station would be located. Sonny diligently worked on the construction of the building and the purchase and installation of the latest electronics as they became available over the years. Sonny would take a moment and stand in the back of the main weather center and watch the technicians in action. Each time he would remind himself that the original construction began nearly forty years ago. Since then the footprint had expanded to include a Doppler radar with its big white ball, more office space, and a larger launch area for releasing weather balloons.

Of the ten employees that kept the operation working 24/7, Mellissa quickly became Sonny's favorite. He marveled at her enthusiasm and the joy she brought to work every day. "I can't remember anyone like her. She's one-of-a-kind," he told Pops Bellman at a Rotary meeting one time.

The sky cleared and the sun appeared behind puffy cumulus clouds as Mellissa came off her shift. Her time card read 14:18. and she was in a hurry. Mellissa and her sister, Cindy, were meeting for a late lunch at their favorite bistro, The Gathering Spot, a short distance from the hospital where Cindy worked as a nurse intern. She was in her third year of nursing school and figured to graduate in the Spring.

Mellissa looked in her purse for her car keys as she backed her way out the front door entrance to the station. Just as she turned to go, Sonny held the door for her. "So, you've decided to leave on time today," her boss asserted as he brandished a big smile. Mellissa did a half twirl and waved as she ran for her car. "Got to go, I'm having lunch with Cindy." Sonny waved back, shaking his head as he entered the building. He knew that the two Bellman sisters were close and rarely had the opportunity to meet during the week, because of their conflicting schedules.

The head of operations at the station walked through the main corridor and entered what Sonny proudly referred to as "The Flight Deck". This was his latest designation for the room where big decisions were made as weather disturbances rolled from the Pacific Ocean toward the Cascade Mountains and over into the flat, sagebrush covered lands of central Washington State. It was the end of August and the jet stream tended to come mainly from the southwest, providing warmer conditions to the region. As the seasons turned to Fall the jet stream would shift to the north, giving the Northwest more cool, even frigid, temperatures to contend with from October through April. In their forty years of weather service, there had been very few variations in the weather. Some years saw more snow in the winter, but nothing too disturbing. Central Washington was known to have warmer and more stable conditions due to the mountain ranges that sheltered the area and blocked most of the heavy weather threats.

Sonny worked with his team to analyze not only the current weekly forecast, but the long range forecast for winter as well. The region's farmers and ranchers depended on his personal predictions more than the Farmer's Almanac or the National Weather Service reports. Little did they know that Sonny used both resources in making his final forecasts. Recently, he told the Flight Deck crew, "Looks like we'll have a wonderful Labor Day weekend coming up. Keep working on the long range, I'm concerned with some of your thoughts on how climate change may throw us for a loop this winter."

§

Business at Magic Trucking had been fairly steady in the early years. Pops Bellman started the company with one service — hauling whatever customers wanted moved. And that became a challenge. Pops found himself agreeing to transport whatever the client needed moved. You name it, Bruce Bellman hauled it. Everything from roadkill to cow manure, necessitating some quick cleanups before the next round of jobs.

In his first year, 1979, the country, especially rural communities like Moses Lake, Washington, were ready for change. America had been through gas shortages, war, the replacement of a President and an uptick in illegal drug use.

Bruce and Maggie were determined to start a family and build a life in Moses Lake. As Maggie put it, "We want to celebrate raising a family in this place for years to come." One way she celebrated was decorating for every major holiday, especially Christmas. Bruce enjoyed helping Maggie decorate as their family began to grow as did the hauling business.

Even in his younger years, Pops would begin his day with a farmer's breakfast consisting of eggs, over-easy, toast, white bread, bacon, crispy or sausage, big links — and coffee, black. Maggie would be ready at six a.m. to share a prayer and eat together before feeding the children by seven. Pops would be out the door by 6:45 to do chores before work, switching to Magic Trucking business depending on a slowly increasing business schedule. The Magic Truck wasn't far from home, conveniently located in the west side of the barn.

As the workload grew, Pops had to hire help in order to balance farm and hauling schedules. Neighbors helped out until Pops was able to afford a five acre parcel with an existing garage and warehouse formerly owned by the Burlington Northern Railroad. The site was a perfect fit and became the official home of The Magic Trucking Company in 1984.

The eighties were a time of growth for many small businesses. Rural communities in Central Washington were known, primarily, for their farming and ranching, especially when it came to apples, sugar beets and potatoes. The introduction of wine vineyards added to the area's agricultural impact and brought more migrant labor into communities like Yakima, Ellensburg, and Moses Lake. Along with the new labor force came the downside effect of drug trafficking, which also had to be monitored along with the weather. Moses Lake became a "stopping off" point for traffic along Interstate 90 traveling east and west.

Eventually, Bruce "Pops" Bellman became a community leader through his involvement in various civic organizations around Moses Lake. One of his favorites was co-chairing the Downtown Moses Lake Christmas Festival with his wife, Maggie. For the last decade he alternated his volunteer time between driving the float that Santa rode on to actually wearing the red suit himself.

The decades seemed to fly by as the Bellman family increased, the Magic Trucking business became an important part of the community, and the Bellman name became synonymous with civic pride.

In his last year of participation, having moved up from driver to acting the part of Santa for the previous ten years, Pops promised his family that he would keep the Santa suit as long as grandkids kept coming. His family loved his energy and the way he carried himself, tall and proud, into his later years.

Pops became famous for his ability to talk his way in and out of any situation life tossed his way — that would never change as he faced retirement head on. The Chief of Police in Moses Lake, Harley Morris, once told a downtown rotary audience that Pops Bellman had more ways to talk himself out of a speeding ticket than anyone he stopped in his 20 years on a motorcycle. "One of his best was back when we were both younger and Pops was building his hauling business. I stopped him for going 45 in a 30 along Lake street. When I told him he was going 15 miles an hour over the limit he said: ' You know the speed limit is 30 and I know the limit is 30, but my customer doesn't care. All my customer knows is that he needs this load by 10 this morning or he's out of business.' I just looked at him as Pops Bellman began to blow his nose and fake a cry before he continued with the kicker, ' You don't want to put the poor man out of business now do you, officer?' The rotary audience was in stitches by the time Harley caught his own breath and lowered his face closer to the microphone on the podium, finishing with, " I let him go." Cheers erupted as Pops, encouraged by his table mates, then stood and took a bow.

Bruce Bellman couldn't help himself. He looked forward to meeting more people and helping his community out whenever the need arose. And as the years passed, age was just a number as far as he was concerned.

Pops, a nickname that began in his family and eventually found traction throughout the community, never paid much attention to the trucking business bottom line as long as he could put food on the table and keep a roof overhead. But in the last two years, since his boys became more involved, business increased steadily, especially over the last 18 months. Current year-to-date figures, January to August, were up nearly 27 per cent, thanks mainly to his son Peter's attention to detail and a new focus on that all important bottom line.

Peter felt the warmth of pride come over him as he closed out of the Microsoft Excel accounting spreadsheet he'd developed and took another drink of water. The end of August had been unusually warm, but he and his family welcomed the opportunity to enjoy the surrounding lakes and trails. He chuckled to himself thinking that working the accounts could actually dehydrate him. Peter swiveled in his office chair, stood and looked out his office window, satisfied with the new company logo he'd been working on with a local design firm. It featured the letters *MTC* above the spelled-out name of the company, Magic Trucking Company, painted on his pick-up, a cargo van and a 20-foot box truck. The use of vinyl lettering had become hard to maintain, especially during extreme weather changes. Replacing letters had become a routine job more and more often. As business improved, Peter saw an opportunity to implement the new logo using newer technology. He also envisioned a whole new fleet of trucks based on continued increases in business.

Peter could feel the pulse of their business beating faster in all areas: Moving, storage, and delivery. Gone were the days of hauling roadkill. The new computer operating system allowed him to track the three revenue streams much more efficiently, which required a bank loan extension in anticipation of new revenue. As long as the revenue kept coming there would be no problem paying the additional $150,000.00 balloon payment on a proposed two million dollar bank loan. The payment would come due in the Spring on March 31st. Peter had it all figured out. Since taking over from his father, Peter had implemented new strategies as the business emerged from COVID-19's darker days. Customers, new and old, were more than eager to relocate to a new location or upgrade equipment, and that worked well for companies in the moving, storage, and delivery business. In addition to six 26-foot delivery trucks, a new computer system, six laptops and monitors, and four new employees assigned to work in a new 25,000 square foot steel building dedicated to freight. Storage containers would be stacked outside alongside a small fleet of three new heavy duty cargo vans. The vans will be used for smaller moving projects for apartments and condos, while the twenty-six foot trucks will move three- to four-bedroom homes and large offices. It was a stretch for the company, but Peter remained confident in his decision to move ahead with the bank funding. *No risk — no gain.*

Last week, after dinner with his family, Peter returned to work with the promise to be home before midnight. He worked the computer analyzing the past five years of data in preparation for a presentation he would be making to their bank in the morning. It became imperative for The Magic Trucking Company to remain in a growth mode and ahead of competition beginning to show up, especially from Spokane. Peter could feel the pressure, but he was determined not to let anything slow them down. His proposal provided MTC with enough cash flow to extend their service area into three new counties and, hopefully, keep their record sales climbing.

Beyond the funding, another critical part of Peter's plan hinged on family, mostly his two brothers and the four contractors that worked for them part time. They had to accept the fact that there would be more work coming and be willing to increase their work schedules to accommodate this new business. Pops would also be available on an as needed basis. The brothers knew that retirement did not sit well with the old man, but Maggie had something to say about that. She always knew what was best for her Bruce.

Next on the list of challenges Peter needed to confront had to do with his older brother, Michael. He loved Michael and admired him so much. Peter, and everyone that knew Michael, understood that the family's first war veteran needed time to heal mentally as well as physically. Peter found it difficult to watch Michael force himself to come to work — on time and ready to go. In less than six months, Michael's return went from war hero to struggling vet going through the motions. He would show up to work just to please his father and family. The hope that he would snap out of his malaise soon diminished into simple frustration for all parties, especially Michael. The fact that someone had to pick him up and drop him off didn't help Michael's attitude. Peter could have hired someone to take Michael's place, but then what? How would that affect the one person he had hoped to please the most in life-the multi-sport high school and collegiate athlete with better than average grades and all the dates one guy could want. The protector. When Peter found himself being bullied at school, one conversation from his older brother and the bullies disappeared like a star filled sky at dawn. Michael just smiled in amazement when a young Peter gave him the good news about being able to walk home from school without a worry. "Imagine that, Pete. They must have other things to do." Then Michael would take his little brother to the Liberty Bell Cafe for a root beer float. Michael always seemed to know how to make life just a little better at the right time. Now it was Peter's turn.

Chapter 2

Chet almost forgot that he promised to call before the delivery. He needed to look for her cell number written on the back of a Wendy's napkin that he left in the glove box of Old Reliable. He watched for a wide spot on the shoulder of the road where he could pull over in order to conduct his search. Thankfully, he found a shady spot a couple of miles from the Hawthorne Ranch and parked. He watched a farmer till along a hillside at a steep angle, thankful to be in the delivery business and not on that tractor.

The deep glove box required a light to see all the way to the back. With his cell phone battery down to 29%, Chet decided to use the company flashlight. He had to reach under the driver's seat for the long black-handled light that had to be as old as the truck. He flipped the flashlight on — no light. "Really?" It took more than a few hits on the butt of the light before a warm golden glow appeared. He scanned through various papers, a glove, some old gum wrappers. *Where is it?* After a few seconds the white napkin with Wendy's face appeared with the phone number blended in under the stain of green hot sauce.

Missy had been on his mind since he made the first delivery of Christmas decorations to the Hawthorne Ranch. Missy answered right away. "Ah, so you remembered to call — that's a good sign." Chet hesitated. He didn't know exactly what she meant by the comment, causing a delay before telling her he was ten minutes away. "Great. Whew. For a minute there I thought you had driven off the road." She met the truck at the usual spot near the barn on the Hawthorne property. Chet still couldn't believe how big the ranch was when he made the turn onto the long driveway. The second time around allowed him the opportunity to get a better look at one of the largest homesteads he'd ever seen. Chet stood on the tail gate of the truck while Missy rounded up one of the ranch hands to help unload the delivery. He watched cattle grazing across the road to the west as horses ran free on the east side of the road having been released from their stalls in the big barn. Further east and south a tractor worked at harvesting an alfalfa field; a smaller tractor pulled a converted trailer loaded with food and beverages for the field workers. It was close to noon as workers began lining up along a concrete slab with portable bathrooms and, what the Hawthorne's referred to as the chuck wagon, near the barn. The chuck wagon was outfitted with a small bell that the driver rang at mealtimes as she did for lunch. They had been working all morning, according to Missy, harvesting a large field of beets at the far southern end of the Hawthorne property. Chet watched the people gather as he slowly drove closer toward the barn and began the process of backing up. He could see Missy standing with a man in the rearview mirror. The man waved the truck closer to the loading dock until he raised a closed fist indicating for Chet to stop. Chet shut the engine down and jumped out the driver's side, slammed the door and began unloading his last delivery of the day.

The delivery went on without a hitch until Chet turned to have Missy sign the delivery sheet he retrieved from the cab. There she was, standing in the glow of the morning light shining through a tall maple tree that stood nearby. Missy looked like an angel guarding the ranch. Chet smiled because he knew this angelic figure could bust a bronc, rope a calf, and help run one of the largest ranches in the Central Basin. He wondered in that moment if she also knew how to do the two-step and line dance, a personal favorite pastime of his. That momentary thought caused him to miss a step as he exited the truck, a maneuver he did several hundred times a week.

Chet suddenly found himself doing a weird version of the two-step when his right foot missed the truck's running board. Missy's gloved hand went to her mouth trying to hide the smile that began to appear on her face. Meantime, Chet did a balancing act consisting of a few bending and twisting moves, hands up overhead, trying not to fall directly into a horse's water trough that sat waiting to catch him. Missy and one of her associates watched the unexpected show, along with two cowhands training a horse in a corral nearby, and the man helping to unload the truck. *Slick moves delivery guy.* Missy didn't know whether to cheer or scream as her delivery guy danced his way across the lip of the big tub, landing flat footed on the other side.

"Lose your balance there, Chet?" Missy couldn't hold back from laughing, as did the young lady standing next to her with a bouquet of fresh cut flowers. "Nah, just my cap and a little pride." He bowed to his observers with a toothy smile that showed through the dust he'd kicked up. The two ladies caught themselves staring at this klutzy hunk a few seconds longer than necessary.

Chet walked around the trough, retrieved his Mariners baseball cap, dusting himself off as he went. He ran a hand through a full head of shoulder-length blonde hair before replacing his cap and asked Missy to sign for the delivery. Now it was her turn to be impressed with the way the man appeared through a cloud of dust as if he'd just ridden in on his horse after a long ride on the prairie. "Ah, sure. Here you go," Missy uttered as she looked up into the bluest eyes she'd ever seen. Chet smiled at Missy and looked over her shoulder at the young lady standing next to her. "Oh, Chet, meet Maria. She and her father, Geraldo, have worked the longest with us here on the ranch. They organize a group of seasonal workers for us each year from Mexico City." Chet nodded to Maria, who stood a little shorter than Missy in a flowery summer dress and sandals. He also noticed she had a slight bulge in the front of that dress. Chet smiled at both ladies as he folded the signed delivery sheet and tucked it in his back pocket. Maria looked down at the fresh-cut flowers in her hands, waiting for someone to do or say something. She knew Missy like a sister, and as far as Maria could tell, Missy was taking more time with this handsome stranger she'd referred to earlier as *her delivery guy.*

Finally, without another word being said, the three walked slowly toward Chet's truck. Chet removed his cap and started slapping dust off his pants and looking around as their walk slowed. The ranch was different from others he'd seen. It had been laid out with an exacting purpose, like a patchwork quilt that his mother sewed with her *stitch and bitch* buddies. He couldn't get over the variety of patterns from the fields of waving crops to cattle and goats grazing on light brown slopes, and floral gardens, featuring large orange and white geraniums, in rich dark soil set closer to the main house. All the patches were outlined by bright white fencing, making the patterns even more defined. He watched as a dozen people spread out working in a field to the south, which prompted a question. Missy had a look of relief as Chet turned to ask.

"How many people work for you?" Missy looked back in the same direction as Chet before responding. "Between the ranch work and the field work we have 20 green card employees from June through November." Only Maria and her father, and two others, actually live there on the ranch year round. The rest live a mile further down the main road, closer to town, in a small complex during their six months with us before returning to Mexico.

They traded smiles as Chet adjusted his cap. He had a full schedule and needed to go, the truck had six more stops to make and it was almost one o'clock. He'd been rehearsing in his mind what he would say to Missy about getting together sometime, but the right words refused to materialize in time, besides, it didn't feel right to put her on the spot in front of Maria. Chet knew one thing for sure — he felt different when he was around Missy. *Get in the darn truck.* He decided to call Missy later as he reached for the truck door and mounted the step up into the truck. That's when he felt a blow to his bum. Spinning around he came face-to-face with Missy. "Well, cowboy, you goin' to ask me out or not?"

Chapter 3

Enrique sat in a straight-back chair listening to Senor Morales. The men in the alley had escorted him to a white stucco building that served as the municipal center for Nogales where five others, including Morales, sat waiting.

"Enrique. Enrique. You are someone who has a future, a very big future, if you choose, hijo." The man sat higher on the other side of a large wooden desk as if he were the Almighty in the flesh. The god-like figure had four men sitting, two on each side, behind the desk. Enrique recognized the man next to Morales as he watched the god's lips move. Patch, a name the vendors gave the hard-looking, stocky street boss, kept the vendors in line and made sure payments to the "City" were on time.

After about a minute, the lips stopped. "Hijo? Are you listening to me?" Enrique immediately froze with fright. He hadn't been listening close enough, and now it was his turn to talk. He cleared his throat twice, then offered, "Yes…senor." It was all he could think to say. Suddenly, Enrique felt alone and all at once concerned for his life. Señor Morales looked directly at Patch, then, after a few beads of sweat appeared on his forehead, back to Enrique with a slight smile. "You…you need to agree with what I just presented to you, hijo… the opportunity to work for us in the United States." Enrique looked up from staring at his hands and smiled, but the look on his face deceived him. Morales could tell his pick of the vendors hadn't heard a word of his carefully rehearsed rhetoric. Still, there was something about

Enrique that appealed to the old man, so he quickly recapped what he'd said while Patch made notes. The second time around made it clear to Enrique that he pretty much had no choice but to go along. There would be no going back to his street corner.

Enrique knew that others before him had disappeared — here one day and gone the next with no good-byes. He had been tossed into the same muddy current by being given a brief glance at the darker side of Nogales. He had been thinking of changing from the daily grind of selling to tourists — he should think of this situation as an opportunity if he was to survive the night. Enrique nodded his head in agreement. Morales pushed his chair back and reached forward to shake Enrique's hand. The eight men in the room all stood and escorted Morales out the back, all except one — Patch. Enrique had just agreed to travel north to the State of Washington and meet up with a contact that worked for Morales at a place called the Hawthorne Ranch.

Patch told Enrique to sit back down. The stocky former wrestler looked over-powering in a black tank top as he pulled a chair close. "You work for me, understand?" All Enrique could do was nod. "We are compadres and I will guide you, starting with this." The man handed Enrique a folder. "Read these instructions now, commit them to memory before leaving this room. Do not make any notes." Enrique spent the next hour memorizing names, routes and one phone number. He was given a phone before Patch left him on his old street corner. Standing alone, waiting for a car to show up, Enrique took a deep breath. On the exhale he cried.

§

Michael Bellman wore noise-reducing headphones and dark glasses while relaxing on top of his bed under a thin blanket.

His bed became a familiar cloud he would fall into with the lights off, curtains pulled shut, and a towel shoved beneath the door. The routine became his escape from the real world as the harsh sounds of the day gradually drifted away. Even birds singing outside his window bothered him. They never used to and that bothered him even more as Michael attempted to focus on his former self and not his current status as suggested by one of his therapists. His parents had granted him residence as long as he remained in therapy. "Whatever it takes." His father sadly lamented one day as Michael showed up for breakfast.

Whenever he misbehaved as a kid, Pops would send him to his room. Laying on his bed he felt that same shame he did as a teen. He also felt that life had become an even more stern disciplinarian, sending him to his *go to* place whenever he became upset. A heavily decorated VA counselor suggested he consider taking control of his seemingly uncontrollable actions. Talk about confusion, especially early on in his therapy. But after several months and a steady stream of therapists, he finally worked up enough courage to ask questions. Michael credited his newest therapist, a female officer, who spent time in the Middle East, with a breakthrough. She understood Michael and what he'd gone through, because she had gone through the same challenge herself after three tours. When Michael asked how long he'd have to retreat to his room for comfort, she softened her voice, looked at his chart and replied, "Allow yourself to let go of the military and go home to your family. If you do that, Michael, you will find yourself in a new place as a person that is more comfortable with where you are now. Maybe the time is now — only you will know when the time is right."

He lay there, in total blackness, feeling as though he had been cast off from what he knew and tossed, against his will, into an unfamiliar void. It had been a little more than six months since he'd been home, discharged with honors. *What did that even mean? He had so many questions.* That feeling of nothingness, would it allow him enough space needed to deal with what's honorable in life? The one memory he hated most came to him in a rush. His face wrinkled as the image of an older surgical nurse with kind eyes appeared. She stood over the triage bed he'd awakened to find himself in, causing him to gag in surprise. Michael was trying to catch his breath while she was carefully attempting to comfort a soldier with a severe wound.

It had all happened so fast. Joking with his buddies, the explosion, screams, and now silence as he lay in the field hospital staring up at a stranger. Her words echoed as she spoke, "You've lost the lower part of your left leg." She wiped away the tears that formed in his eyes once the echoing stopped and he understood, but she could do nothing about the sobs that followed. Instead, she leaned forward, closer to the left side of his head that was not bandaged. In a soft, almost motherly voice she whispered, "Michael, it's not what happens *to* you — it's what happens *in* you after a traumatic injury that matters."

With that thought in mind, his brows pushed together as he tried to focus on what his life was like before signing up to serve his country. He'd been so busy trying to survive the last three years, he realized he could never switch back to his life before bunkers, bullets, and bombs. Turning inward to find a new life was more frightening than facing the enemy.

Removing the headphones and pushing his dark glasses up on his head, Michael pulled back the familiar green curtains in his room with the large orange and yellow sunflowers. The sunlight immediately hit the silver and copper colored trophies lining the wall on the other side of the room. The impact of light caused tiny dots to dance around the room, finally landing on pictures of a younger Michael interspersed with the trophies he'd earned. The older Michael would sometimes stand and stare at that younger version of himself until tears formed or voices in the house interrupted him. This was his room, that person *is* him, but he couldn't relate to any of it. He knew he'd come home, but why? Some that served with him vanished, never to be seen again, except in dreams. The one therapist he liked the most said that the trauma of survival continues through blame. The fact that he blamed himself for not doing enough when his crew perished in the explosion deepens the hurt. Michael had a new fight on his hands. It was called: Post Traumatic Stress Disorder, PTSD. Knowing he had a condition was the first step to healing. At least that's what the doctors felt comfortable discussing in front of him. Their diagnosis didn't match what Michael believed. He wondered how many of the professionals treating combat soldiers actually had any *hands-on* experience. Did they really understand what it was like to be a target in the enemy crosshairs? Or witness a friend dying next to you as survivors pull you out from under an armor-plated Humvee. You can't hear what they are yelling because the concussion affected your hearing, but you knew the platoon was in trouble and there's nothing you can do about it. Helpless, you slowly blackout as the medic's medication takes over, slowly eliminating the pain that had finally begun to emerge. Those moments that you had feared could happen, because of your commitment to the Corps, become the only dreams your mind will allow. From that moment on you will not be granted permission to remember or reflect on happier times. When will it stop, when will my mind become mine again?

Michael's heart beat faster as he floated in the darkness thinking about the explosion and hearing the screams from his crew. He coughed and began to choke. Automatically, he reached for water, took a drink and slowed his breathing by taking deep breaths. He didn't know how long it took, but eventually it happened. One breath after the other, holding for four seconds in and out, until his heart rate returned to normal. It was becoming a little easier. Deep breathing relaxed him, helped him look inward. Eventually, his physical wounds began to heal to the point where he'd begun to work out. Maybe it was time for his mental wounds to do the same.

Michael removed his headphones from his shoulders with his left hand and the sunglasses with his right. All of sudden he didn't want to continue to lay on the bed. Michael threw his right leg over the edge of the mattress then the left, but there was no left leg. *What the?* The momentum from both hips moving across the bed sent Michael directly to the floor. He lay there in the dark, face down, on the hardwood floor. He made a mental note to move the throw rug closer to this side of the bed. The thought made him laugh to himself. "Son-of…" before he could finish, a burst of laughter left his lungs, flushing out whatever he held inside.

He laid still on the carpet contemplating his next move—his life really. A surge of energy hit him, beginning in his feet. He could feel his left leg as if it was there, toes and all. *What's happening?* He had to move. Michael rolled to one side and pushed away from the floor. He stood and immediately began to fall to his left, catching himself before hitting the night stand by bending his good leg. He looked straight across the room to a figure in the full-length mirror. *So that's what a bent-kneed, one legged, long haired idiot looks like!* A deep primal growl came out of nowhere and Michael started to hop in place, which made him feel silly all over again. He started laughing to himself and soon he was moving toward his temporary prosthesis, which the night before he'd thrown across the room placing a slight dent in the wall. *He'd have to fix that.* As Michael scanned the room he noticed the chair and his artificial leg. *Move.* Once he had the new limb in place, he realized he needed to eat something. How long had it been?

Maggie answered the phone on the second ring. "Good morning, Peter. Yes, your brother is still here — I heard him growl a few minutes ago. Oh, umm, I'll explain when you get here. You may need more than coffee, dear, but I'll have it ready." She hung the phone up not knowing what was about to happen between her two boys. Michael had been doing his best to fit in, but lately he acted like a complete stranger. Poor dear.

The door to Michael's room upstairs nearly came off the hinges as he bolted for the stairway. "Mom? Are you here?" "Yes, dear. Are you alright? I heard a growl." "No, I"m not. But, I am hungry."

Maggie watched in horror as the former track star hurdled high over the stairway banister, nearly losing his balance, but regaining it just in time to land, on his good leg and one hand, at the bottom of the stairs with a resounding "Yes!"

"My goodness, Michael. What's got into you?" "Mother, I'm tired of sleeping and feeling sorry for myself. And if I don't get something to eat soon, I'm going to pass out." Maggie fought back tears as she grabbed her apron and hurried to warm up Michael's breakfast of eggs and bacon. She made toast and put her award winning strawberry jam out along with orange juice. Michael ate as if this were to be his last day on earth. "You might slow down a bit, dear." Maggie used her apron to wipe her eyes as her oldest son did his best to eat more slowly between gulps of juice.

Pops kept himself busy outside by cutting wood for the fireplace in the family room. The weather was beginning to turn and soon it would be Fall, which meant cool mornings and he wanted to be prepared. The old tree stumps came from his neighbor's farm located about twenty miles south of Moses Lake. Pops helped the elderly man take out fallen trees and clean up around the place. The man had allowed Pops to use two of his out buildings, an old barn and a garage for storing trucks and equipment in the early days of the trucking business.

Pops had to hurry. He'd lost track of time — as usual. He and Peter were meeting for lunch at the house to go over some business questions regarding MTC's bank status. As Pops entered through the backdoor of the mud room, located just off the kitchen, he heard Maggie laughing. After quickly washing up he entered the kitchen with a question. "What's so funny?... What the heck?" Sitting there and eating an extremely large portion of bacon, eggs and pancakes was Michael. "Hey, Pops, join us, we're having breakfast." Pops sat slowly at the end of the table just as Peter walked in with almost the same look on his face. "Mike, you're up, eating — breakfast!" Michael's response came quickly, "Pete, you always were the smart one. I know it's lunch time, but mom talked me into having breakfast instead." Michael looked at his mom and winked. Maggie dabbed her eyes with a tissue as she turned away and said, "That's right, Peter, we're having breakfast, anyone have a problem with that?" Both Pops and Peter shook their heads and agreed that breakfast sounded just great. And so it was that the three men sat together eating breakfast for lunch as Maggie joyfully continued to flip pancakes and fry bacon.

Chapter 4

Since she could remember, Cindy Bellman dreamed of becoming a nurse. In pre-school she would go around the house collecting bandaids, cotton balls, an Ace bandage, several small plastic containers, and a magnifying glass that doubled as a stethoscope. She kept all the items in an old purse her mom had placed in the Goodwill box after too many years of use. The purse matched a blue leather handbag that Cindy kept an eye on just in case it, too, would be tossed. Cindy loved the softness of the blue leather with a gold clasp. It had a strap long enough to go around her shoulders with the bag bouncing off her knees as she walked with purpose through the house on her way to provide aid to a make-believe patient.

Once Cindy reached middle school, Maggie would take her along when she volunteered in the hospital laundry. Twice a week the Ladies League organized the collection, washing, and folding of blankets and clothing for newborns and toddlers who were hospitalized. Cindy was in seventh grade when she was allowed to tag along on Saturday mornings helping to accomplish as many tasks that a twelve-year-old could handle.

The hospital seemed like another world to her. The smells that ran through the hallways bustling with people coming and going were very different from those at school or at home, until she reached the laundry room. Apart from the enormity of the gymnasium-sized facility and the largest washers and dryers she'd ever seen, those sounds and smells were more welcoming to her. The clanging and banging of the machines mixed with

the bleach and detergent combined to make things cleaner —
better. As it turned out, Cindy was not only good at the tasks
in laundry, she gladly helped stock shelves, where the clothes
and bed linens were kept, by watching the nurses and how they
handled their various duties. She idolized a few of the younger
RN's, especially those who worked in the Operating Rooms,
because they wore special outfits that covered their entire body,
including their face. Whenever she and her mom would take
a break and eat in the cafeteria, Cindy would look for the OR
nurses. One morning, a surgical nurse noticed Cindy watching
their table. She'd noticed the cute sandy-haired girl several times
before, walking the halls with her mother. The nurse smiled at
the wondering girl. Cindy quickly looked away, but when she
looked again the nurse was walking her way. What happened
next would change Cindy's life forever. The nurse sat down
after introducing herself and by the end of a short conversation,
had invited Cindy and her mother to sit in the main operating
room's observation area with her. They watched together as
other nurses prepared the room for the next OR patient. The
nurse, and Cindy's mother, were impressed by the questions
that seemed to naturally flow from the excited child. "Do each
of you have a specific job? How come the doctor stands there?
How long do operations take?"

Cindy also had an opportunity to visit the Emergency
Room when she broke her leg while snow skiing with her family
at Mission Ridge Resort. Peter had challenged her to try skiing
down a black diamond run. "She was lucky," her mother said
later. "Cindy could have broken her silly neck." Cindy's older
brother felt terrible and accompanied her in the ambulance
to the hospital. "Don't worry, Michael, I've always wanted to
ride in an ambulance," she told him as they both broke into
laughter. After all the chaos surrounding the day, Cindy came
to the conclusion that she would like to be a nurse one day, but

not in the ER. It was too hectic for her. She needed to be in a place that worked within a more controlled environment.

As the years went by, Cindy decided to pursue her dream of becoming a Registered Nurse, specializing in Pediatrics. She enrolled in a new program that divides her time among attending classes, working in the hospital, and studying online. The program began in Spokane, a city located an hour and a half away in eastern Washington and known for being a major hub for healthcare services. Cindy commuted for six months before finding an apartment to share during the first two years of the program. She would make the drive home on the weekends to catch up with family and share stories about working in the pediatric center at Sacred Heart Hospital in Spokane. Cindy's current schedule keeps her closer to home and working in a hospital she knows like the back of her well-washed hands. She had another two years to go before graduating with a Bachelor in Science degree before taking the Registered Nurse exam and looked forward to that day.

For now though, she was running to meet up with Mellissa and enjoy some sisterly girl-time over lunch.

Chapter 5

It didn't take long for Michael to get back in step with his brothers. He finally reconciled, on his own, to stop feeling sorry for himself. His top priority became to focus first on healing with family and friends. The hurt feelings of the people you chose to be close to in life are the hardest to repair. Michael knew that and prepared himself for whatever happened. Close behind healing with people he cared for most was the fact that he needed to get into a healthier routine of eating and exercise. Hopefully, returning to work with a better attitude would be the kickstart he needed to get his head on straight and go for it.

Michael spent part of a year in limbo after coming home. Like most athletically-gifted teens, Michael once dreamed of becoming a professional athlete. Pick a sport, he excelled at whatever he tried. Coaches built reputations on kids like him. Football and baseball were on equal footing, but baseball, his personal favorite, topped the list. When he found his old baseball cards stuffed away in the closet of his old room a few days ago, he wept. Everything the therapists and his family had been suggesting, all at once, made sense. Waves of anger and frustration gave way to a plain and simple realization that had been patiently waiting in that old cigar box. *You can never go back to who you once were. Your best option is to move forward.* Drive is a difficult gear to engage when you are stuck in reverse. He didn't know how long he sat at the bottom of his closet. But when the crying subsided, he knew the weeping wasn't for who he was now, it was for that kid who once dreamed of following in the footsteps of Ken Griffy Jr.

Later, when Chet found out about his older brother's transformation, he summed it up with a snap of his fingers: "It was as if he went from black and white to full color, just like that." Chet wasn't the only one to notice. People around town shook his hand and waved when Michael showed up in public with that all familiar smile they were used to seeing on the sports page years earlier.

One Saturday afternoon Michael stopped by his former high school's practice field to watch the coaches work with the varsity football team. His coach had stopped by the house, more than once, to visit and Michael had declined to meet with him. Michael made a promise to himself to make this visit a priority. When his former head coach saw him coming he blew a whistle and had the players gather around. The embrace and the interaction that followed with the players that day made Michael feel as though he'd scored the ultimate touchdown.

He found out from the coaches that day that his former baseball coach had died while Michael was serving in the military. Driving away memories of Coach Phillips working with Michael after practice, hitting grounders and pitching until dusk for batting practice came flooding back as he headed to the cemetery. But first, he made a stop at a florist shop.

Within two weeks Michael rode shotgun with Chet, making deliveries and moving freight around the warehouse after teaching himself how to drive the forklift with a newly fitted foot replacing a smaller one on his prosthetic leg. The wider foot made a huge difference, especially because he had to push from his hip to work the floor pedals of the forklift. He cleaned out the trucks after deliveries and worked alongside other employees catching up on all the various jobs at the Magic Trucking Company before taking that seat next to Chet.

Michael considered himself as the *utility guy*, someone who did whatever needed to be done, whenever. It was his idea and Peter agreed. As they hugged in Peter's office, he recalled the rant Michael threw a few weeks earlier before storming out of his office. Peter smiled as he listened to his older brother. "I've been slacking off and I just want you to know I'm back and want to work," Michael told Peter that morning at the breakfast/lunch. "I'm ready."

Since then it was as if Michael had become a different person. He continued with his semi-monthly therapy sessions and his medication for PTSD. It seemed as though he'd fought through the morass of self-loathing and climbed on top of the dark wave that had threatened to overtake him. Instead of drowning, he pushed back and refused to let it happen. Peter's facial expression radiated pride and relief. This was good news and it came just in time. "We can sure use you big brother."

In an effort to demonstrate his change in status, Michael shaved his shaggy months-long beard and began to work out after his physical therapy sessions. His goal was to gain back his muscle mass in order to be fit and ready to do his job at work. His workout sessions were scheduled for three times a week at a local veterans outreach center run by a former Marine staff sergeant nicknamed; Goliath. The black man cast a big shadow at the facility standing six foot six and weighing around 250 lbs. with long dark hair that curled down past his shoulders. The most impressive feature on this giant of a man was his leather eye patch dotted with silver studs. To anyone who asked, he'd say that he lost the eye doing too many push ups with two people sitting on his back. *Never found the eyeball though. It's around here somewhere. Do me a favor and keep an eye out for it.* The big man had an even bigger sense of humor, a massive gut wrenching laugh, and the ability to get the most out of anyone he coached. According to him all students had to do was try.

Goliath's real name was Kenneth Richards and he lost the eye in a knife fight in Kandahar, Afghanistan where he guarded the American Embassy and participated in night patrols. Sgt. Richards led a night patrol of eight, highly-trained, soldiers through dusty darkened streets searching for their target — a sniper who was making life in the embassy extremely difficult. The situation dictated that the *mark* had to be eliminated without alarming the entire neighborhood. The order for *knives out* became the priority. Sgt. Richards split the group in half, sending four soldiers around the back of a suspected apartment building. He and his four soldiers went to the basement and worked their way up going door-to-door. The incident happened on the fourth floor where the sniper was having dinner with another man behind a tarp in a dark corner near a balcony. The five soldiers surged forward with Goliath in the lead. According to Goliath, it happened in a flash, he took one in the face as he and the sniper traded blows. The sniper's long rifle and the other man went over the edge of the balcony as Goliath turned to face the sniper. The force of Goliath's first strike started in the enemy's gut and ended up in his neck. He covered the target's mouth with a large bloody hand and felt the victim's muffled screams down to the victim's last breath as Goliath carefully laid him down on the stone floor.

Later that night Goliath called home and talked to his mother. He sat alone in his tent. Goliath's watch read two a.m. The call went through without a hitch. It was dinner time in Alabama and his mother would be preparing the dinner meal for Kenneth's father and four siblings that remained at home. His mother, Ruby, had the reputation for fixing hearty meals, especially at dinner time. The land line phone rang three times before Ruby answered. After the initial scream and the thank you's to the Lord above, she asked, "Kenneth, are you okay, son?" He assured her that he was fine. He just needed to hear her voice. They talked as she passed on the dinner duties to his younger sister, Jolene, 13. "You do what you need to do in order to come home in one piece — you hear me, son?" Goliath loved her loving reassurance that he felt he had a special duty to fulfill. It took a load of worry off his shoulders to know that everyone was okay at home. Even though the conversation didn't last more than 15 minutes, because of his location, that was all he needed as he thanked her and she blessed him.

Goliath and Michael shared more than one story, allowing each to let go of that darker past with each telling. The sharing created a bond between them that neither man had anticipated, but greatly appreciated. The kind of storytelling that only happened between veterans of war, never with curious civilians in a bar or more importantly, with family.

Michael shook off the rain as he walked into the VA center ready to workout with the man he now considered his friend and coach. Michael's work clothes were neatly packed in a black vinyl bag he placed in a locker just as Goliath came around the corner. It was nearing six a.m. and they were the only two in the place. "Morning, Mike. Hey, before we get started I just want to apologize for last night at your place." Michael looked up at the big man and smiled. "My family loves you, man." The night before Goliath showed up for Sunday dinner at the Bellman's family home. Michael asked his parents if it would be okay to invite a friend from the VA Center for Sunday dinner. "Of course," they both said in unison. His mother wondered if Michael had met a young lady, his father didn't care. It pleased Pops to see a smile on Michael's face as he reached out and made new friends.

When the giant of a man walked into the Bellman's home that Sunday the whole place stopped moving. It was like watching one of those movies where everyone suddenly stops whatever they were doing at the same time, some with their mouths open, and others frozen with raised eyebrows. Most members of the family had heard Michael talk about his coach, but they'd not met him — until now. All eyes were on the handsome black man with an eye patch who appeared to bend down in order to get through the front door. Goliath caught on to what was happening right away and half whispered to Michael, "This is your parents' house, right Mike?" Michael shrugged his shoulders as he and his invited guest proceeded forward. All eyes around the table remained in surprise mode.

All eyes remained fixed on the front door, except for Maggie's, as she entered the dining room from the kitchen. Maggie was mumbling something about the dish being hot as she continued toward the table with a large plate of mashed potatoes to compliment the roast beef sitting in front of Pops who had just made the first cut, but had suddenly stopped. Chet, Mellissa, Cindy, Peter and his wife and son, were also in a frozen state. In spite of the looks on his family's faces, Michael made a quick introduction. "Ah, everybody, this is Goli…ah, Kenny, my workout coach." Maggie finally looked from her husband to the front door. As was her style, Maggie didn't hold back, "Oh, my," came out first and then she added, "We're going to need much, much more… of everything." Kenny looked at Michael, hit him on the shoulder, and began to bellow out a deep hearty laugh. The big man's response caused the whole house to erupt in laughter. When the surprising burst of laughter finally died down, Kenny walked over to Maggie and politely taking the plate of potatoes in hand, asked her if she had any for the rest of the folks gathered around the table, which resulted in a second round of laughs. By then, Pops had stood to meet the gentle giant of a man holding the plate of potatoes. As introductions were made, Cindy and Mellissa couldn't take their eyes off the mountain of a man who made his way to the table, sat directly across from them mid table, and gave them a wink. Both girls did their best to keep their composure.

Giant echoes of laughter could be heard on the street outside the gym as Michael and Goliath sat on the same bench laughing as they relived the night before at the Bellman's. Michael could not recall a time when his whole family was at a loss for words at the same time, with the exception of his mother. When the laughter finally subsided, Goliath had a question. "Hey, Mike, I want to get your opinion on a Christmas decoration I've been working on." Michael looked at the big man as he walked off toward his office. A few minutes later he came out with a sketch of a wreath with the USMC logo and Merry Christmas inscribed on a large red ribbon that ran through the wreath, ending in a bow. "I like it." Michael said. "Great. I'm going to order several and hang them here and down at the recruiting office around the corner."

People began to stream in for Goliath's first workout session of the day, which included Michael.

Chapter 6

Mellissa walked out of the morning meeting concerned about the long-range weather forecasts for possible extreme winter storms. She stopped and looked up at the panel of six 52-inch monitors that stretched across the main office area, needing to get some clarity. Here they were in early September and already the forecasts called for a winter season of La Nina-like weather patterns. She tried to imagine what that would look like as she continued to gaze at the monitors. From where she stood, Mellissa overheard Sonny asking Bridgett to coordinate the write up of a long-range weather prediction for the media to broadcast. "The local television stations want to compare the Farmer's Almanac to what we come up with this year." Mellissa knew that the media liked to make the comparison every year, what she didn't know was who kept track of the National Weather Service versus the Farmer's Almanac. She also knew that Sonny didn't appreciate being challenged, but went along with the request. The man, besides being a great boss, was also a good sport. Moments later, Mellissa felt a tap on her shoulder.

"Mellissa, here you go." Bridgett handed Mellissa notes from the meeting and suggested she check with the National Weather Service for any back up information they could provide regarding seasonal forecasts due to climate change.

"Sonny wants to review what we come up with by tomorrow morning." Mellissa nodded her head and walked immediately to her desk. She enjoyed a challenge and knew she'd be working on the assignment for most of the day.

Later that afternoon a sudden rush of wind came blowing through the main work area. The source of the heavy breeze came from the back door of the station. Slam! The heavy metal door hitting its frame made the walls shake. "Watch out, coming through." Mellissa looked up in time to see Rod, one of the other forecasters, rushing in the back door all muddy and apparently quite upset. Every afternoon at four o'clock a second weather balloon of the day is launched. The first having been released 12 hours earlier, just before sunrise. Fellow employees sitting close by looked away, trying not to laugh. But Mellissa, feeling sorry for the poor guy, felt compelled to say something. "Trouble with the balloon launch, Rod?" He looked at Mellissa as if she had just spoken in a foreign language. "Trouble? Trouble? My whole life is just one large, deep, unforgiving pit full of trouble, Mellissa." Muffled laughter could be heard as she rushed to find a clean towel in the janitor's closet. "Hang on Rod." She finally located several blue colored towels and handed a couple to Rod who proceeded to clean off his glasses and wipe his face. "I don't suppose there's a change of pants and some boots I can wear in that closet." Mellissa just stood silently looking at her unfortunate colleague as he proceeded to scrub away the mud that had accumulated, not only on his glasses, but down the front of his shirt and pants. "I'm sorry, Mellissa, I didn't mean to take my anger out on you. Thank you for the towels." She nodded at him as they returned to their desks.

Mellissa felt sorry for Rod whose last name, Lingo, had become a target for jokes from some of the crew. It didn't help that Rod happened to be one of those clumsy people who dropped, fumbled, and tripped more than the average person. In the last few months an expression had become synonymous with Rod's misfortunes. Some of the guys would urge one another not to pull a *Lingo*," or worse, "Did you see that the

Mariners *Lingoed* in their loss to the Red Sox last night?" Rod tried to be a good sport about them associating his name with an accident or mistake. Mellissa felt anyone would get extremely frustrated when things didn't go well, like falling in the mud or walking into a wall while reading a report — as Rod would do routinely. Evidently, someone had left the hose running outside after washing the windows earlier in the day. The water ran down the path used to launch the weather balloons creating a muddy bog. When Rod went to launch the balloon, he looked up at the windsock, which is required, then walked directly into the unexpected mud pit. As the balloon ascended, Rod tripped and went the other direction, falling, face first into the mud. "*Splat!* I couldn't even track the balloon leaving the area, Mellissa."

Before Mellissa's shift was over, Rod came by her desk. He thanked her again for her help. "I was able to wash most of the mud off my face and clothes. How do I look?" Mellissa had to be careful as Rod turned completely around in her cubicle. She noticed that the leftover mud had dried causing a crust-like texture on his shirt and pants. He looked uncomfortable, so she quickly nodded and whispered, "Better." Rod assured her that he was fine. "I'm off in a few minutes anyway." Rod looked over the top of the cubicle as a couple of guys sarcastically gave him the thumbs up sign. He adjusted his stance and lowered himself as he pulled out some papers from his crusted back pocket. "Hey, did you see this on the long range printout?" Rod showed her an unusual weather disturbance forming over the Bering Sea off the Alaskan coastline. Mellissa could tell that Rod was uncomfortable after reading the printout. He had a look of concern that she'd never seen. "I've been watching that area for the last six weeks, Mellissa." She didn't know it, but Rod had a contact located in Alaska, an uncle, who managed a weather station further north. "My uncle said there have been some abnormal weather patterns that have an added intensity to them that are considered "Highly Unusual." Shipping traffic has been alerted, causing some delays in normal fishing, container freight, and cruise travel. He's been in this business for almost two decades and has never seen anything like it," Rod's uncle admitted.

They talked for a few more minutes until Mellissa asked Rod to leave the information with her. No one else in the station appeared to share their concern. They hadn't seen the look on Rod's face. Mellissa was into details. The more she thought about what Rod said about the weather pattern up north being unusual the more she wanted to know about it. But first, she had to make sure that there was something to be concerned about. After all, the information did come from Rod. In addition to being accident prone, Rod did have the reputation around the office for taking things to the extreme. Forecasting weather was more like a religion to him. For everyone else, except Sonny and Mellissa, working in the weather center was a job. Mellissa smiled as she tucked the printout carefully under her desk pad with the top corner sticking out. She'd had a long day and looked forward to two days off.

As Mellissa walked to her car, she noticed Rod knocking his shoes together on the back porch of the station. He suddenly stopped, noticing her watching him. He managed a smile and nodded, nearly falling off the porch. He replaced the loafers on his feet as he walked, stiff legged like the Tin Woodsman in the Wizard of OZ, all the way to his car. Mellissa let out a sigh after watching him, turned the key in the ignition, checked the rearview mirror, and slowly pulled away behind Rod's car. She couldn't help but feel sorry for the poor guy everyone seemed to pick on, but she understood. Rod Lingo knew more about meteorology than the average forecaster and didn't hesitate to share. That didn't sit well with most of the other guys. Mellissa and the other women understood Rod's need to socialize and went out of their way to be friendly to him. What she didn't understand was printed out on that sheet he'd given her. Mellissa stopped the car and turned it around and headed back to the station. She suddenly needed to review that long-range printout. She wanted to know what her mud-caked colleague had been so concerned about — and why?

Chapter 7

Missy invited Chet to join in the festivities surrounding the decorating of the ranch for Christmas. After all, he offered and she never turned down anyone who volunteered to help, especially someone as good looking as Chet Bellman. There were two annual holidays that the Hawthornes decorated for: Christmas and the Fourth of July. Christmas was the bigger of the two of course, and required weeks of preparation that Missy and her brother, Tim, shared in managing. At least that was the intention. Missy admitted that she couldn't do her part without the *very capable* assistance of Maria. Together, they ordered all the necessary materials such as; lighting, ornaments, wreaths and other essentials that either needed to be hung in just the right location, repaired, or used in new ways around the ranch. It seemed as though someone was always coming up with a new spot to decorate around the ranch.

Tim and Geraldo handled the execution of hanging lights, wreaths, garland and any other materials approved by Jake Hawthorne. A few neighbors helped with the exterior work in order to meet the ceremonial deadline. Chet felt a little out-of-place as the newest volunteer to join in the holiday preparation. He showed up early one Saturday morning, as instructed, ready to do whatever was necessary. It felt odd to him — decorating for Christmas in September, but he was willing to go with it.

Chet headed toward the barn where Tim and two of the ranch hands were loading boxes of lights into a black GMC Denali pickup truck with the Hawthorne Ranch logo neatly displayed on the cab doors. "Morning." Chet waited patiently for Tim or one of his men to acknowledge his greeting. After a minute or two Tim finally turned around in Chet's direction. Missy's brother nodded his head at Chet as he placed a clipboard on a stack of boxes and jumped from the loading, taking off his gloves as he walked in Chet's direction. "Missy said you were coming, Chad is it?" Chet smiled, cleared his throat and corrected him, "Chet." They stood looking at each other as Missy's voice came over the walkie-talkie clipped to Tim's belt. "Morning boys. Hi, Chet." Chet followed Tim's gaze toward the large picture window in the main house where Missy stood waving. Chet returned the wave. A second later Tim gave him a slight punch in the shoulder and started to walk back toward the loading dock. "Come on, we've got work to do."

Missy, Maria and a few of the neighbor ladies, handled the interior decorating. Missy had her hands full planning decorations for Fall, Halloween, Thanksgiving, then Christmas. Each seasonal change had to be followed according to an outline that her mother developed years ago. The Hawthornes loved the changing of the seasons, which was easier when the ranch was smaller. Missy promised her father that nothing would change as long as she, Missy, was left in charge. Even as the ranch grew. What she didn't plan on was keeping an eye on her brother who had trouble showing up on time because of his drinking.

In the last few months, Tim's dependence on alcohol had gotten worse. He had been in therapy since the helicopter crash nearly two years ago that took his mother's life. He had been piloting the helicopter the day of the accident and managed to survive the fiery crash, suffering only minor injuries. Lillian Hawthorne had been so proud of her son's ability to learn the difficult task of piloting their Bell Ranger helicopter used to survey ranch operations. Missy's father also leased the copter to the local authorities for search and rescue operations. Lillian had also been taking flight lessons, and was capable of flying with an instructor. She had every confidence in her son who manned the controls that fateful morning.

The shock of losing their mother could still be felt, but Missy and her father seemed to be the only ones who had decided to move on in order to keep the ranch life Lillian was adamant about developing — alive. Tim continued to struggle with survivor's guilt as it was explained to Missy and her father. No one knew how long it would take or if he would ever recover, but the hope that he would was always there. In the meantime, Missy told her father that he could depend on her to do whatever it took to keep her mother's memory alive, which included the Hawthorne ranch life.

Chet was one of six volunteers gathered around Tim and Geraldo as Tim outlined the work for the morning. "My father wishes to thank each one of you for helping out this year. Before you ask, the answer is Yes. We are starting the decorating earlier this year than in years past. The reason is — we have more trees to decorate. Plus we have more ranch work to do this year before our help from Mexico returns home after the Fall season. We will be hanging lights in the trees that line the driveway, starting in the courtyard and working our way to the front gate — 30 trees in all. " He pointed to the two ranch hands and Chet, "I'll take you three with me and work the south side, Geraldo will take the rest and work the north." Geraldo added, "Remember, we're stopping at noon because we have other work to do this afternoon." This was a major part of the total work with the goal being to have the outside decorations ready by Thanksgiving, a little less than two months away. Missy watched as the Denali, loaded down with boxes of commercial grade multi-colored two-inch lights, twelve-inch crystal snowflakes, various sizes of metal clamps, and green colored extension cords, left the barn area heading for the top of the driveway. Standing inside the ranch house at the living room picture window, Missy excused herself and took a short break. She told the ladies inside that she had to check on the driveway work, which was partially true. Missy also wanted to see her delivery guy in action.

Besides, she enjoyed his company. She secretly wanted to watch him go up and down the ladder wearing those tight jeans she'd seen him wearing during the last delivery he made a week ago.

Missy looked around as she walked. She couldn't help but feel her mother's presence as memories of her parents organizing the holiday work came rushing back. After her mother's death, Missy waited, patiently, to see if her father would want to continue with their family traditions. When she finally worked up the courage to ask, he reached out and held both of her shoulders and gently whispered, "Yes, of course, my dear. It's what your mother would want us to do." His following hug felt especially warm that day.

Missy knew that bringing the ranch to life with lights everywhere was something her father looked forward to all year and Missy loved watching him take charge. Jake Hawthorne had the reputation of a hard-driving *get the job done on time* kind of boss. But Missy also knew he was a big kid at heart when it came to holidays, especially Christmas. She somehow needed to find a way to introduce her father properly to Chet, the *magic man*. Who knew Moses Lake could kick out such a handsome desperado? There was something special about Chet that made her smile whenever she thought of him. That feeling for someone beyond family was new for Missy. All her life she wore the label of a rebel. A Tomboy. It made her feel closer to the ranch, her father, and what she thought made her special on the ranch. Who knew that choosing to be with a person could be so…exciting. Especially if they choose you back.

Pride began to build inside her as Missy walked closer to where the men had begun working. Her father joined the group on the north side of the driveway and was talking to Geraldo. She saw Chet go with her brother, so she headed in that direction. Tim appeared to have things under control as he showed Chet how to hang the lights properly. She didn't want to interrupt, so she kept walking. A cool late September breeze came up suddenly and it felt so good. The wind brought a strong smell of pine with it. Thoughts of managing housekeeping, meals and ordering supplies, work her mother did so naturally, came to mind. "Mom, help me be more like you," she whispered into the wind. A feeling of confirmation wrapped around her suddenly. Her walking stride increased and she began to jog. Eventually, she broke into a full run and she continued to run, glad she had changed into her running shoes before leaving the house. Thoughts of helping her father manage the ranch, scheduling the ranch hands who cleaned the barns, worked the cattle and maintained the landscaping raced in her head as she ran along the fence line. She never knew how many day-to-day challenges one person could face, but Hawthornes had the reputation of being a tough, well-organized breed. Besides, her mother raised Missy to be self-sufficient. She missed her mother's positive attitude and gentle touch. Tears began to flow as Missy remembered when she was little and had both her mother and big brother to lean on when she had a problem. Back then, her father was a different story. He dedicated himself to turning a small farm into a working ranch, beginning with a 50-acre homestead that eventually grew into just over 10,000 acres to date.

She passed the one mile marker on the fence with no thought of stopping. The fence line became a blur and Missy couldn't contain herself as she let out a loud primal shout. She did an internal check as she ran. Everything was in good shape. No pain and lots to gain. *Keep going.* Missy smiled as she surpassed her previous single run mileage and turned back up the driveway. She blew a kiss to Chet, who held two fake snowflakes up to his ears, as she ran past. Missy stopped short of the barn and began to cool down before returning to the ranch house and a hot shower.

Missy's pride in her family, especially her father, showed whenever she smiled. Friends and business associates of the Hawthorne family often remarked at how much Missy reminded them of Lillian. She devoted herself to do the best she could to help fill that gap created in her life. Making that happen and carving out a life of her own kept her guessing about her future.

Later that afternoon Missy's phone buzzed, it was Chet. Even though she wanted to hear his voice, she let it go to voicemail since she and Geraldo were going over tack inventory. After a minute her phone buzzed again signaling a voicemail had been left. A short time later, inventory was accounted for and put away. Missy smiled as she and Geraldo left the barn, each heading in different directions. Geraldo went to check on cattle grazing in the east pasture, while Missy checked for messages.

Chet put his phone away after leaving Missy a message, confirming his participation in the holiday decorating for next Saturday. He almost ended the call then added, "Your brother had a piece of advice for me that involved you. He said he'd kick my ass if I ever hurt you. I told him you could probably kick both our asses, so he didn't have anything to worry about." Chet's response completely surprised Tim, who nearly fell out of the tree they were decorating, he laughed so hard. Tim lightened up after the incident, asking questions about Chet's family. The two men got along after that and made good progress on the decorating. As a parting comment in the phone message, Chet wanted to know if Missy ran cross country in high school. "I had a great view of your run this morning. You really turned it on." Now it was her turn to laugh as she pressed the call button.

Chet did his best to stop thinking about Missy as he checked his Saturday afternoon delivery schedule, but now found moving on into work mode a challenge too. Peter had asked him to help make local deliveries in Moses Lake, every other weekend, on an as needed basis. Chet agreed and thought the additional workload would serve as a distraction and give him more time to come up with a way to ask Missy out. He had never known a girl like her and it made him unusually nervous. *No wonder I'm nervous — she's not a girl, Missy Hawthorne is a woman.* The question in his mind became clear — was he ready to become a man?

He found the next address and pulled the van into a commercial loading space next to the courthouse when his phone rang. *It's Missy.*

Chapter 8

Yura silenced the alarm on her digital clock and rolled out of bed. This particular morning came early because it was her turn to walk the family dog before leaving for her first class. Yura was 19 years of age and entering her second year at Ilisagvik College, a public tribal land-grant institution. Her grades were better than average, she enjoyed most of her classes, and she made the Dean's List. Yura felt good about her direction in life. Living at home helped her save money in order to find a place of her own in the coming year, possibly out-of-state. Most of her friends who attended Ilisagvik College, a small college in a small town,lived at home. The good news was her college had a great reputation for academic achievement.

Yura hoped to pursue a career in oceanology and help to clean up the oceans of the world. The University of Washington in Seattle had a program, but living expenses there were beyond what her family could afford. Yura remained undeterred, she had a plan and promised herself that she would make it happen, on her own, by excelling in school.

She used her headlamp to guide her through the house as she jump-walked putting on her socks and workout pants as she made her way over the thick wool carpet. The family dog, Panuk, a big blue-eyed Alaskan Husky, waited patiently at the back door as she sleepily approached. Yura worked late at the weather station the night before and found herself stumbling more than usual as a result of staying up late. She yawned as she readjusted her headlamp while reaching for the dog leash. She loved her five year-old companion who danced before her, refusing to act his age. "Good boy, don't worry, I'll let you run once we reach the pier." Her parents encouraged Yura, the oldest of four children, to trade walking Panuk with her younger sister, Atka. Yura would take the winter days and Atka the warmer summer months — June through August for sure and September if the weather held out. The rest of the family would take the remaining months of the year.

Yura knew that the day would warm to a high of 27 degrees Fahrenheit, as she quickly finished putting on her outer gear and boots. But that was a few hours from walking time with Panuk. For now, the two companions would deal with near freezing conditions. Yura felt the colder temperatures and extended time together brought her and her dog closer than anyone else in the family.

The six a.m. fresh snowfall matched Panuk's hairy coat making it appear as though Yura was holding on to a leash with only the collar visible in the limited light. The thought made her smile as the sound of crunching feet on snow could be heard as they left the yard through the back gate. The roadbed was hard-packed with early snow, a forewarning of what was to come. Even though there was a history of snow year-round in Utqiagvik, the new snow came with surprising intensity this year. The thought of snow triggered a conversation she had the night before at the weather station. Yura listened as the station manager attempted to explain, as best she could, strange happenings in the atmosphere. Climate change became the villain as her manager went on and on about the possibility of continuous atmospheric rivers that had the potential to cause devastating catastrophes. "Conditions that would be difficult to predict and even harder to recover from."

Panuk stopped to pee and Yura nearly fell over him, lost in thought in the darkness, and holding the leash connected to the invisible canine. "Sorry, boy." She laughed to herself as Yura untied his leash and let him run the last block to the pier. Yura wound the leash tightly around her arm, automatically adjusting her headlamp band on her head as she carefully searched for Panuk, finding him waiting on top of a log next to the pier. Panuk let out several barks to let Yura know he was waiting for her.

Dark clouds began to mix with lighter grays as the sky began to lighten up from the ocean's horizon. The marbled layers swirled together over the ocean that bordered the shores on three sides of her city as Yura handed Panuk his favorite treat made of cornmeal and dried fish. She couldn't take her eyes off the streaking showcase of finger-like patterns that appeared to beckoned anyone watching to pay attention. Darkness quickly gave way to various shades of gray clouds and dove into the ocean, seemingly pushed by the soon-to-rise sun.

The two companions walked side by side, both watching the sky lighten as they made their way along their usual route. The varying shades of gray blended perfectly with small dots of white as the sun refused to show itself, hiding under a white curtain just above the horizon. The darker gray clouds slowly swirled overhead and away like a hand waving good-bye over this part of Alaska that covered precious oil deposits, sea life of all sizes, and fellow citizens who preferred to exist among the vast and dangerous beauty of the region. Yura never felt so small and stumbled on the formerly familiar shoreline as she watched the sky perform in such an odd manner.

The former Barrow had had a larger population and

footprint only a few decades earlier. Decisions that limited the production of crude oil extraction in the area may have reduced the size of Barrow's population, but not the need for oil. As the conversation over fossil fuels and their impact on the environment continued, the climate's reaction went seemingly unnoticed, except in places like Alaska where glaciers were slipping away in record numbers only to disappear altogether. As discussions over what to do about rising tides, firestorms, and floods continued, so did the climate respond in the only way it could — as it did now.

Yura wondered if the dark clouds that surrounded her that morning were the first of many atmospheric rivers that were forecasted to be gathering this winter season. Yura hurried as she snapped the leash on Panuk, which was uncharacteristic of her. She led Panuk home as the wind made a hissing sound as if to tell Yura not to share what was to come. Yura looked up to see Mother Nature in the clouds, holding a slender finger to her lips. Nature had another response to climate change in mind and she wanted it to be a surprise. Of all the natural disasters related to the changing climate, this one would be special for it would arrive in time for the holidays.

Yura kicked off her boots and held tight to Panuk as they watched the sky together from the safety and warmth of her home.

NOME, ALASKA — REGIONAL WEATHER STATION

The October/November weather forecasts were beginning to show signs of several unusual disturbances, one after the other, coming closer together in frequency, which caused the station manager to pay closer attention. The rhythm of expected weather patterns suddenly became historic memories as a new normal began to show itself. Even though it was mid-September, he could tell the atmosphere had become more of an unfamiliar entity looking to cause trouble.

Climate change had been responsible for more than usual spring rains and intense summer storms earlier in the year further south in the Pacific Northwest. The station manager's concern, upon reading the most recent forecast, became; What would winter be like for residents in southern Alaska, western Canada, and the Pacific Northwest? Most of the cities, including airports on the coast in Washington and Oregon shut down when snow levels exceed six inches. The reports he read, especially one out of their northernmost station at Utqiagvik, called for the extreme possibility of flash freezing ice followed by snow amounts higher than ever recorded. The cause focused on atmospheric rivers, which would have a domino effect through Alaska, over western Canada and into Washington State, east to northern Idaho and possibly Western Montana.

He sent out the alert to all station managers in those areas and then made a personal call to his nephew, Rod, in Moses Lake. He often checked in with his nephew by email, his favorite nephew, because Rod chose to follow in his uncle's footsteps as a meteorologist. But, rather than just an email, this disturbing weather information deserved a phone call.

Rod Lingo placed his muddy clothes carefully in the wash, as if they were contaminated with some foreign substance. His arm stretched out as far as it would go before releasing each item. After his shirt, a favorite, pants, socks and underwear were safely deposited, he lowered the lid, pushed the appropriate buttons, listened for the water to kick on, then left, wrapped in an oversized bath towel. After his bath, he dressed in his bedroom, putting on his workout sweats before sitting down at his computer with a cup of hot green tea. Rod made sure he performed each movement in logical order, trying not to waste time or cover his tracks more than once. After taking a slow sip of tea he began reading through emails and stopped when he came to the one from his uncle. Rod set the cup of tea down slowly, not even looking at the saucer. Just as he finished reading the last sentence, his cell phone rang — it was his uncle.

Chapter 9

Chet turned the radio on in his Dodge Ram pick up. He had the windows down and the music up as he left the freeway heading for the Hawthorne Ranch. This was the first time he wasn't making a delivery or helping out with the early Christmas decorating. It had been nearly a month since meeting Missy and he finally had the time and the courage to ask her out. They would be headed to Billy's Country Inn, the biggest western entertainment venue in the Northwest, for some barbecue and line dancing.

A new set of nerves showed up at the same time Chet made the turn into the courtyard of the Hawthorne home. The place was unusually quiet for an early Friday evening he thought as Chet made his way up the flagstone steps to the front doors. He started to ring the horseshoe shaped doorbell when he heard Missy's voice from behind. "Hey, Chet. Sorry we were busy with a new calf bein' born this afternoon. Finally made it." Chet couldn't believe his eyes. Missy was covered with dirt, hay and what looked to be an oily liquid. She caught his look then added, "I know, I'm a mess. Listen, you talk to Daddy while I get ready." Chet smiled and followed his cowgirl date into the house where a Tamarack fire warmed them the moment they entered. Missy turned and asked Chet to wait by the fire. "I won't be long, Maria went to fetch my father." Missy hurried off while Chet looked around the stone and log interior with twenty-foot ceilings. Tan colored tile covered the floor from wall-to-wall. A large white furry throw rug lay between the fireplace and tan colored leather furniture. Just as Chet was beginning to sit in what looked to be the most comfortable chair in the room, Maria appeared. "Chet, good to see you. Is there something I can get for you?" He asked for water and she let him know that Mister Hawthorne would be in shortly.

When Maria returned with the water Chet thanked her. She noticed that he'd been looking at a large painting of the Hawthorne family hanging above the fireplace. Chet made a comment about the beauty of Missy's mother. "Miss Lillian was the most beautiful lady…" Maria hesitated, then began again as Chet looked at her, "We all miss her very much." Maria smiled and excused herself and Chet could hear a deep throated voice coming from another room. Chet looked back at the painting and was able to put the voice to the face of a dark haired man with tan, very striking features, a goatee with a nice smile. Jake Hawthorne had intended to meet Chet before, but life and business took priority, at least for the time being. He also had another reason to meet the young man — the youngest son of Pops Bellman. Geraldo had also talked about Chet and the fact that he seemed to be a hard-working young man. A comment that every father liked to hear. Jake always looked out for his daughter, like any father would do. But his fatherly duty in that respect had been fairly easy because he knew for sure — Missy could take care of herself. Still, he looked forward to meeting Missy's *delivery guy*.

"There you are. I'm Jake Hawthorne. You must be Chet Bellman."

After shaking hands, Jake showed Chet into his office. Jake let Chet do most of the talking. It was Jake's way of getting to know someone without having to ask too many questions. Their conversation quickly turned to sports with Chet listening to one of the most interesting people he'd ever met. They were talking about the Mariners, but stopped when Missy came into the room wearing jeans, western shirt, purple and black; barefoot, holding her boots in one hand and hat in the other. "Almost ready, Chet. Daddy, have you shown Chet your sports collectables?" Jake smiled and looked down at his desk and pushed a button that activated a wall panel that slowly rolled back revealing another room the size of a large walk-in closet. Missy disappeared saying that she'd be back in ten minutes. "Chet, this is the room Missy mentioned. It's what I consider my safe room." Jake chuckled as he patted Chet on the shoulder and motioned for him to enter first. "Amazing," Chet had a hard time closing his mouth. The room was full of Northwest sports memorabilia. Everything from uniforms, pictures, books, to equipment, trophies, another fireplace, a skylight, and a leather recliner. "We won't take the time to go through all this, but at some point in the future, when you stop by, I'll have some stories you might enjoy, Chet." Chet shook the man's hand and thanked him for the brief tour as Missy came in all dressed and ready to eat and go dancing. "I'm starving, let's go delivery guy."

Missy's brother, Tim, watched from an upper floor window as the two drove off. Tim's normal reaction in the past would have been to get drunk and spend the evening with his favorite pal, a vodka bottle, watching sports in his room until he passed out. But not now, not this evening. He decided to do a little socializing at Billy's instead and grabbed his truck keys.

Missy couldn't believe how clean Chet kept his truck and complimented him. "It smells like coffee in here," she mentioned as they left the frontage road and sped on to the interstate heading for Billy's.

They met up with a few of Chet's friends and danced for nearly two hours after plates of short ribs, beans and coleslaw. They both agreed that two rounds of PBR beer was enough because of the drive and work to be done the next day. They also agreed to spend some alone time before calling it a night.

Missy gave Chet directions as they drove to one of Missy's favorite viewpoints overlooking the Yakima Valley. "Come on." Chet was surprised when Missy exited the truck and started walking fast toward an overlook area that projected out like the bow of a ship. The visitor's area had a steel railing and several benches for people to enjoy the enormous view. The night sky was full of stars with a crescent-shaped moon that was playing hide and seek with some spotty clouds. "My mother loved coming here." Missy had tears in her eyes as she turned and walked into Chet's arms. He held her close as they kissed. The night couldn't have been more perfect. They sat on a concrete bench with Chet's camping blanket wrapped around them as the October night chilled. The clouds scattered and the stars began to flicker as the moon dropped slowly in the west over the Cascade Range. For hours they shared deep feelings about family and what matters most in life. Both were the same age, 21, and both had decided to continue to work in their respective family businesses. College was not a priority, at least not in the near future. It felt good to finally give in to what they both had been feeling. Neither one wanted the night to end until Missy turned to Chet and asked if he could feel his butt. They both laughed as they walked stiff-legged back to the truck. "I've got to get you home. We're hanging more lights in a few hours."

Missy stood in the kitchen after waving goodbye to Chet. She was checking messages on her phone when Tim surprised her. "Tim, what are you doing up?" He didn't answer right away, instead he asked, "You two looked good on the dance floor tonight." As he spoke he reached out for his sister. They embraced and Tim, who towered over his sister by nearly a foot, began to cry uncontrollably. Missy handed him a tissue and waited for her brother as he wiped his eyes. She began to say something, but Tim motioned for her to stop by placing his index finger to his lips. "I want you to know something."

He stood and walked to the other side of the kitchen island. He leaned in with both hands on the top of the island and said, "I'm going away." Missy wanted to say something, but Tim kept talking. "I talked to Dad and he agrees that I need to check myself into a rehab center for alcoholics in Tucson, Arizona." Missy felt a sudden rush of relief and almost lost her breath. She nearly fell off the island chair as Tim came rushing toward her. He held her by her shoulders and asked if she was okay. "I…I don't know what to say, Tim." The two of them talked about the arrangements that had been made and that he would be leaving, later in the morning.

Tim apologized for his reclusive behavior since their mother died. He blamed himself for the accident and wished that he'd never survived. He admitted that his insistence to fly the helicopter that she accompany him that day caused their mother to give in and go. He also admitted that he made a mistake in flying too low and fast, when they hit the powerline. "I have to live with that, which I'm willing to do — I want to live and become a more productive member of our family. Missy and Tim talked through the rest of the night. Neither one wanted to say goodbye. She loved her brother and told him so as he and his father left for the airport in the morning.

§

The holiday decorating went off without a hitch. Missy had everything well-organized as expected. Her mother would have been so proud of her *Missy Girl*. Chet felt a little self-conscious as he directed the cherry picker up to the peak of the barn. Missy took him up on his offer to steer the picker and she was not about to say no, in fact, she was relieved. Chet had worked on more than one roofing and construction project using Magic Trucking Company's cherry picker.

Attached to the base of the basket was a very large green wreath decorated with lights that Chet and Ricardo, a ranch hand he just met, were about to install on a black angle iron that was now pointing straight at them. Missy and her father watched as Chet skillfully maneuvered the picker with the ten-foot circular wreath hanging from it. He had to make sure the wreath didn't start swinging freely as they closed in on the target.

"Every year the wreath seems to grow larger, Missy. That new angle iron that Ricardo installed should handle the load." Missy's father watched his daughter's face as he spoke. He could tell she really cared more for the operator of the picker than the load factor on the angle iron.

"Over to the right a little and down about a foot," Richardo directed as he reached forward with the attachment line. A big silver clip needed to fit over the curve of the angle iron, first, before the wreath could be pushed backward against the barn wall. "Steady, steady… that's it! Now push forward." Chet pushed the glide handle forward until he heard a clicking sound. "Stop." Ricardo put his thumb up and smiled at Chet.

When Chet and Ricardo returned to the ground, Missy was there to greet them. "Good work, guys." Both men pushed right-handed knuckles at one another as they stepped off the picker, Chet went first. He stopped to look back at what he and Ricardo had just accomplished and caught Ricardo looking the other way, toward a corral by the barn where a man stood in the shadows. The dark figure lit a cigarette, blew out the first inhale as he motioned for Ricardo to join him. Ricardo looked a little nervous as he thanked Chet for his help and was off. Missy walked closer to Chet and put her arm through his. "Chet, my father wants to talk to you, he's inside the house in the den. I'll join you in a minute." Chet seemed distracted. "Did you hear me?" "Huh? Oh, yeah. Hey, who's that guy over by the corral?" Missy looked where Chet was looking. "That's the new guy, Enrique." She went on to explain that Enrique had been hired by Geraldo, the ranch foreman. Enrique's job will be to assist Ricardo with some new field work that Missy's father requested. Chet thought it was just a little odd that Enrique acted like he was the man in charge, but quickly lost the thought as Missy gave him a shove. "Get going cowboy."

Chet laughed as he faked a stumble, dusted off his blue jeans and flannel shirt, stomped his Bass boots as he walked from the front of the barn and into a flagstone covered courtyard the size of a tennis court. The sun had just begun to set over the rusty-orange colored stones, which triggered a string of small golden lights, hidden in the vines intertwined above his head, as if to show him the way.

The front door stood halfway open like a large welcoming hand revealing the inside of the Hawthorne home. Chet slowed his gait as he passed the full-length letter "H" carved into the oak plank with a large black iron handle with matching hinges.

A huge chandelier hung overhead as Chet entered into a world of oak in the most beautiful log home for the second time. Not that he hadn't seen it before, but the sight amazed him, once again, as he looked up into twenty feet of endless wood with white chinking. Maria greeted Chet from across the room, standing on a small ladder washing the dining room window. Chet returned the greeting as he continued toward the den.

"Come in, Chet. Join me in my inner sanctum." Chet looked to his left at the man who gave him a brief tour a few weeks earlier. Missy's father stood with a dark brown drink in his hand and a smile on his face that made Chet feel a little uneasy. Chet reminded himself that he really didn't know Mr. Hawthorne that well and that he should just relax and listen. Mr. Hawthorne, who stood a couple of inches taller than Chet, had the reputation of being a hard-driving tough negotiator, according to Chet's father. Referring to Missy's father one day, Pops Bellman explained how members of the Moses Lake Rotary remembered the imposing figure and hearing Jake Hawthorne give a speech to their club years earlier, before Mrs. Hawthorne's death. Chet hoped that those old impressions had changed as he followed the man inside his cave.

Chapter 10

Enrique Mara had the reputation of having things his way. From the time he could run with the bigger kids, in Guadalajara, he learned quickly how to survive. He couldn't depend on parents or relatives to teach or defend him — they didn't exist. Enrique knew he had to be faster, smarter, and eventually, stronger in order to live. At an early age, the barefoot urchin caught the attention of a volunteer relief worker handing out meals in a park near downtown Guadalajara. Enrique showed up hungry and in need of medical attention. His abrasive attitude landed him in a fight with four other kids, two of whom wanted to rearrange Enrique's face. A knife had been used to cut a line from the corner of his mouth up toward his right eye. The wound was deep and he held a dirty towel to his face as the worker questioned him. Enrique passed out before she could find out the who and why a deep gash had been carved into the boy's face. The volunteer rushed the boy, she guessed to be 10 years of age, to the nearest emergency room where Enrique received treatment. The older woman stayed with the boy, who remained unconscious for two days.

On the third day after his surgery, Enrique finally awoke in a hospital bed with a stranger holding his hand. His face hurt and he had bandages that covered most of his head. The stranger, a woman, introduced herself and explained what had happened. Fortunately for Enrique, the relief worker had some influence and was able to extend his stay long enough for him to heal from the altercation. The nurses and the relief worker watched as the boy would devour each meal that arrived at his bedside. He had to be coached to slow down in order for his face to heal properly.

It was hard for Enrique to show appreciation for all the attention he received. He tried smiling when the relief worker would stop by, but his face wouldn't allow it. Instead he would wave to her and nod his head when she smiled at him. The day she brought new clothes for him to wear, he knew more changes were coming. Once the bandages were removed and he was able to stand and walk around, the relief worker escorted Enrique to an orphanage supported by UNICEF. She explained that this place would now be his home. They embraced and he held on for as long as he could. Enrique could tell she cared for him because she had tears in her eyes. After a few minutes went by, Enrique made his way up the large stone steps into a new world.

Two years later, and educated enough to read and write, Enrique began to understand more about the world he'd come to know. The headmaster and the teachers took an immediate liking to the young boy with the big scar. He was a fast learner, hungry to know more about life beyond the streets surrounding the orphanage. Over time, he learned enough and devised a plan to head north to seek a new life. He had a long road ahead of him if he were to hike all the way to the border town of Nogales. If he accomplished that he might achieve his ultimate dream of living in America.

After a routine medical exam, Enrique was thought to be 13 years old at the time he left Guadalajaara on his mission to hike north. He also left with a last name, something that had not been given to him since he was born in the ghetto and abandoned. One day during a study group, a volunteer teacher read about a mythical god named Mara. The name translated meant *bitter*. It was also associated with death and rebirth, both definitions stuck with Enrique who immediately decided Mara would become his last name. The organization helped him make it official by listing him as: Enrique Mara, a student in their care. For the next seven months a young teen named Enrique Mara headed north carrying a loaded backpack guided by a strong determination to survive.

By the time he reached the Mexican border with the U.S., he had what he needed to be processed. Although he was not accepted because he had no sponsor, Enrique made connections in northern Mexico over the next five years that changed his life. Enrique Mara was destined to become a key figure in the supply and distribution of illegal drugs coming from South America through Mexico heading for the United States.

For nearly a decade, Enrique Mara, the young street vendor turned drug entrepreneur, was faster, smarter, and in better physical shape than any of his rivals. He had become the perfect example of the ideal drug smuggler. Unlike a majority of his rivals, Enrique Mara kept a low profile, invested his illegal riches, and resided in a modest house on the outskirts of Nogales. He had never been arrested, although the authorities were looking for a man that met his description: Hispanic male, approximately 25 years of age, six foot, short brown hair, light-brown skin, muscular build, with a long scar on the right side of his face. Even so, there were plenty of men who worked the same illegal scheme, Enrique just kept his baseball cap low, and dark glasses clean as he went about his business.

Most people set goals in unison with a career leading the way. That was not the case for Enrique. Every opportunity that came his way, up to this point, *fell from the sky*. That was how he felt. Maybe that was why Enrique became so successful, he never intended to live as long as he had, given how he started out in life. However, since he made it this far, Enrique wanted to take more control of his life by becoming a drug lord rather than a drug runner. He'd been given the opportunity to create his own business with a new drug taking hold in some of the larger cities in America. The opportunity existed in the northwest part of the United States in the middle of Washington State. An area already known as the Yakima corridor for other opioids, but virtually virgin territory for the new drug that would be all his if he decided to take on this new arrangement. He needed to find a way to scout out the location before making his decision. His contact agreed and suggested he make a test run during the upcoming holidays, Thanksgiving and Christmas, when people, including the authorities, may be distracted with other concerns. When he asked what he would be transporting across the border, the answer came with one name, Fentanyl.

§

"So, here's this kid, what were you, seven, eight?" Chet looked at Missy as she watched Pops Bellman hit his story telling stride at the longer version dining room table in the Bellman home. The table had to have both extensions added, which made it about 20 feet long and ending up in part of the living room.

The Bellmans were known to celebrate all through the holidays from Thanksgiving through New Years Eve. This particular gathering happened on the first Sunday in December. All the Bellmans were there and a few invited guests. Michael and Goliath sat facing each other in the middle of the table, Mellissa made sure Rod would be there, and Cindy asked a foreign classmate from England, Chelsea. The British girl couldn't take her eyes off the big black man who sat higher than anyone, smiling and gesturing, across from her.

Maggie created her usual holiday assortment featuring homemade cranberry sauce and scalloped potatoes. And this year she found new people more than willing to help. Maggie recruited several guests ready to lend a hand, including Goliath, who surprisingly knew all about deep frying a turkey, a dangerous but convenient skill he'd learned while serving in Afghanistan.

"Where was I? Oh, yes. We were spending the week after Christmas at our cabin on Lake Chelan." Pops kept an eye on Missy as he retold a family event that nearly burned the old place down because of seven year-old Chet's well-intentioned behavior that morning. "Chet is cold and goes inside to warm up before lunch. Next thing you know, he decides to light a fire in the fireplace. No one happened to be inside at the time, so none of us knew what was happening."

Pops began to chuckle as he slowly explained, with knife and fork lifted high, that once Chet lit the fire, opened the flue, and made sure the fireplace screen was closed, as he had seen the older folks do many times before. He then went to the living room window proud of his accomplishment. He waved to his parents and siblings playing outside until he noticed his father running and pointing back at him. Young Chet immediately turned around and was hit with a gigantic plume of smoke. His father ran into the house, checked the flue, and began to douse the fire with a pail of water. Doors were thrown open, windows, fans, blankets were being waved, people were running in chaos for about the next hour. All Chet could do was stand and watch as the cabin grew smokier and colder.

Pops laughed so hard at this point he could hardly finish the story, "The one-level cabin didn't take up much room on the scenic hillside, thank goodness, so it didn't take long for the smoke to subside, but the heavy burnt wood smell lingered for… years!"

Missy reached under the table for Chet's hand. She was learning more about her handsome friend and she liked it. Chet responded by leaning over and whispering, "Oh, it just keeps getting better." Pops explained that, unbeknownst to Chet, a creature, most likely a squirrel, had built a nest about half way up the chimney. The well-constructed nest completely plugged the standard brick and mortar chimney just above the flue. The family had closed up their family getaway a few months earlier on Labor Day weekend and hadn't been at the cabin since. "Poor, Chet. We couldn't get him to come out of his room until supper. Our well-intentioned son was too embarrassed to show his face." Everyone was looking at Chet, especially Maggie who couldn't help but notice he and Missy holding hands.

Chet let go of Missy's hand, took a sip of water, and sat back with a big grin on his face. He cleared his throat and semi-seriously asked permission to say something. Pops nodded, trying not to laugh, which caused Chet to laugh as he responded, "Of all the stories my father could have told about my youth, he had to pick that one," Chet offered as he raised a glass to toast his father. Missy led the cheers that came from around the table. Pops came up from behind Chet's chair and padded the top of his head, and then toasted Chet with, "Here's to our youngest who is always willing to help, we still love him." Pops then turned and raised a glass to Maggie, "And to our head chef!" Everyone applauded and waited as Maggie stood and encouraged "Our new friends to feel *right at home*." She also suggested Pops quit with the toasts and that they eat while the food was still warm.

§

Enrique walked out of the bunkhouse at dusk after asking for Geraldo's permission to use the side by side ATV. It would be dark soon in the valley and Geraldo hesitated as he sat back in his old leather desk chair. He assured Geraldo that he knew how to drive the high-powered Polaris with turbo capabilities, even though he'd never even heard of one before coming to the ranch. It took a few tries, but after some help from Ricardo, Enrique managed to start and move the vehicle into the south pasture and into an open area the size of ten professional soccer fields. He'd already sent the coordinates for the aerial drop that was due to arrive in 15 minutes.

Enrique turned the engine off, now that he understood, he hoped, how to start it. He nervously checked his watch as he sat ready to blink the ATV's headlights at a low flying aircraft set to arrive. Enrique looked up into the night sky. A jet streaked across the sky blinking red and blue lights as it passed. He wondered where it had come from and where it was going as the plane disappeared into the western twilight. The sound of a far off diesel truck brought him back. His thoughts were racing. He tried to keep his focus on what he needed to do at the moment. It wasn't often that he found himself sitting outside in complete silence. Enrique discovered that he enjoyed the solitude — it gave him time to think more deeply about his new life. He'd never had the chance to experience that feeling back in Nogales. Everything ran at a feverish pitch all day long and into the night and sometimes… sometimes.

Sometimes he wished his life had gone in a different direction. The orphanage was the closest he came to living with people who cared for one another… and celebrated holidays, like Christmas. His thoughts of the biblical birth and the three wisemen were interrupted suddenly. The sound of a far off engine high in the sky brought him out of his memories. He looked for the text from his contact signaling the plane's estimated time of arrival. The engine sound grew louder as the plane descended closer. Enrique had trouble moving the ATV into a more vertical position in order to flash the headlights as instructed. He jammed the gear shift back and forth, finally freeing his ride onto a small slope. He flashed the headlights, once, twice. The aircraft responded to his flashing, slowed, approaching from the south. Enrique watched as the silhouette of a small plane appeared to be making a landing without lights. The passenger side door was barely visible as a parcel with a long white streamer came tumbling out. Enrique waited and watched as a small parachute deployed simultaneously to the sound of the plane's engine increasing in power, allowing the craft to disappear into the night like a cat with wings.

He watched as the package fell slowly onto the newly tilled ground about 50 yards from his position. Enrique powered up the ATV and headed to the landing site. His eyes were on the package more than the ground ahead. He didn't see the slight rise in the ground. A second later he took a hilltop too fast and came down hard as the field went from tilled earth to a series of rocks. A boulder, the size of a basketball, nearly went through the skid plate of the side-by-side. The close call threw him off course and he had to stop to get his bearings. His left ankle started to throb as he spotted the package, a few feet away, with the long streamer on the ground. He came to a stop, limped away from the vehicle and quickly buried the streamer, parachute and lines with a small shovel he'd found in the barn. When Enrique went to stand he nearly fell over on his left side. "No, no, no. This can't be happening." He automatically shifted his weight to his right side, grabbed the canvas covered parcel and hobbled back to the ATV.

Not knowing what to expect, he was surprised at how small the bag was, less than two feet square and not weighing more than 10 to 15 pounds. His nerves bothered him more than his throbbing ankle. Enrique checked all around to see if there were any signs of life — other than the cattle down in the next pasture. If anyone asked, he was just taking a drive to get to know the place a little better.

He couldn't believe that the drop happened just as they planned. He felt good and bad at the same time. A strange feeling suddenly came over him. From this point on he would be responsible for distributing a dangerous drug, on the other hand, he had the potential to make a new life for himself in America. *What's happening to me?* Enrique told himself to snap out of it as he placed the package in a cargo box on the back of the ATV. He looked around one more time before starting the engine. He turned and retraced his tracks, which were easy to find in the dark rich soil.

Enrique's first stop was behind the horse corral where a small lean-to stood in the back of the northside rails. He stached the package containing the drugs, temporarily, in a box that housed the water pump used to fill the horse trough. His plan was to keep the package hidden there, a dry out-of-the-way place, for the next 24 hours.

After returning the ATV he limped back to the bunkhouse for a visit with Ricardo.

§

Chet cleared his throat as he drove Missy home from dinner at the Bellmans. The truck radio was turned up higher than usual on Chet's favorite country music station. And the two love birds started singing along with Toby Keith and his "Red Cup" song, which was the third in a medley of favorites. When a commercial came on, Missy, who was out of breath said, "I think when the next song comes on, you should go low and I'll go high." Chet, who could not stop laughing, had to hold the steering wheel tight in order to keep from going off the side of the road. He had been stomping his left foot as Missy directed the highs and lows in the songs. He replied almost out of breath himself, "We could be much better at this, you know that, right?"

It was now officially Fall, that time of year when the sun continued to set earlier and earlier. Missy loved everything about the season and looked forward to seeing Chet's family and Chet of course. The Bellmans were not fast eaters. Conversation seemed to be the main course no matter what was being served and Missy enjoyed every minute of it. By the time dinner was served and seconds made the rounds there came dessert — Maggie's French apple pies. Their aroma hit the table before the pies did.

In the meantime, the blue sky day had turned completely dark. An evening fog began to make its way down the highway as Chet and Missy headed back to the Hawthorne Ranch. Chet didn't mind the drive with Missy by his side. "So... have you always been that kind of person? Helpful, I mean." Chet knew she wasn't going to let his smoking out the family one winter at their cabin get by without a comment.

As Chet looked over in her direction at the passenger side of his Ford F-150, careful to keep one eye on the road, Missy lifted his right arm and leaned into him. No words had to be said, so there weren't any until Lainey Wilson's song, "Heart Like a Truck", came on the radio. Missy sang along softly. At one point she came out of his hold, leaned back and pointed her finger at him, singing lyrics to the song, "Boy I tell you what, you better... buckle up!" She could hardly finish before they both burst out in laughter, again.

The ride went too fast as far as Chet was concerned. As they turned to drive up and under the Hawthorne sign at the entrance, Chet noticed a set of small headlights bobbing up and down through one of the fields. Missy had her head down looking for her house key. "Did you see that?" he said. When Chet pointed in the direction of the lights, Missy responded. "Oh, that's probably Geraldo checking the fields for some reason." Chet pulled around and dropped Missy off, but not before a good night kiss and a date set for the following Wednesday.

Chet eased the Ford around the courtyard drive taking in all the lighted beauty of the Christmas experience that he helped to create. As he drove toward the tree lined driveway he noticed an ATV coming to a stop. Out of curiosity, Chet put the truck in neutral, shut off the lights and waited. He had a hunch and wanted to see if the person driving the ATV actually was Geraldo as Missy suspected. She admitted that it was unusual for anyone to be going that direction in the south field or any field this time of year, and more to the point, this time of night. Chet watched in his rearview mirror as Enrique came forward out of the shadows walking toward the bunkhouse. *You're not Geraldo, so what's so important in the south field tonight, Enrique?*

Chet chewed on a fresh stick of gum as he started the engine, turned the headlights back on and left, promising himself to find the answer to his question.

Chapter 11

Peter knew he'd stuck his neck out with the bank loan, but the Magic Trucking Company needed the additional funding if they were to stay ahead of the competition. The city of Moses Lake had been experiencing a growth spurt for the last five years. The population increased by 20 per cent due in large part to companies leaving the west side of the state because of overcrowding and the need for more space for land development. The central part of the state had plenty of room for those willing to live further inland in a drier climate.

The balloon payment loomed over him like a dark cloud ready to burst at any moment. By Peter's calculations, the Magic Trucking Company would be able to make the $250,000 payment by the end of March if monthly business revenue increases remained at between 12% and 15% until then, four months from now. In other words, Magic Trucking Company couldn't afford to lose any current business.

Downtown Moses Lake had an updated festive look lining the main streets as Peter drove his truck into the Washington State Bank's parking garage. The Moses Lake Chamber had raised over $100,000 specifically for new Christmas decorations that displayed better in the daytime and broadcast new bright displays that would bring people into the downtown in the evening. "Hey, Pete, how's it going?" Ben Jackson, Commercial Loan Manager for the bank said as Peter entered his office. The two had known each other since high school when they competed together on the wrestling team.

Their meeting at the bank went for half an hour, their lunch at the Broadway Bistro, a place the locals favored around the corner, lasted just over an hour. Jackson was pleased with Peter's numbers, although he also wanted to know how Pops was doing. "How's his health? Is he thinking of retiring?" With each question, Peter understood, Pops Bellman continued to be an important link in the commercial loan chain.

The conversation then led to making plans for a family ski vacation either in northern Idaho at Schweitzer Basin or in northwest Washington State at Mount Baker. They had skied both locations when the Bellmans and the Jacksons took family vacations together years ago, but hadn't returned since.

On the way back to the office at Magic Trucking, Peter passed by the largest nativity scene he'd ever witnessed. The figures were life-size — shepherds, animals, Mary, Joseph and baby Jesus. The display even had the Magi, one of whom was riding on horseback. He slowed down in front of the Presbyterian church in order to take a picture, it was that impressive. He immediately texted it off to his wife.

§

Ricardo sat drinking coffee and looking out the bunkhouse window. He was going over the conversation he had with Enrique the night before. Ricardo had listened to Enrique's explanation about selling a new drug that would make them more money than they ever knew existed.

The new Mexican arrival was physically bigger and came across as a very confident and well-organized person. He felt sorry for Enrique and was upset at the same time. Ricardo was happy doing legitimate work for the Hawthorne family and didn't want to jeopardize his current life by getting into illegal drug sales. Also, Ricardo had relatives who were in prison in

Mexico for selling drugs, so he just sat and listened until Enrique stopped talking and leaned forward. "Well? What do you think, amigo?"

No one else was in the bunkhouse at that time and Ricardo was thankful for that. Ricardo's heart was beating so hard he thought it would pop right out of his chest. *He's still looking at me and wants an answer.* Ricardo had to be careful. The new drug Enrique wanted him to sell had been on social media with warnings: Fentanyl kills people.

"Well, Ricardo?" Enrique prompted. Ricardo smiled and asked if he could take a day to think it over. Enrique's brows came together as his hands balled up into fists before relaxing. "Of course, amigo, take a day. But I need to know tomorrow." He pulled out a small switchblade knife and began to clean it. "And by the way, Ricardo, if you tell anyone about this, well, let's just say, don't tell anyone, okay?"

Ricardo understood completely when he left the bunkhouse last night. Enrique's offer was tempting, afterall, Ricardo was in the United States to make as much money as he could in order to get his citizenship and start a new life. He also wanted to help his father and mother and six siblings in Mexico City. Life was tough these days south of the border, and it didn't take much money to change life for the better there. But soon he would have two more mouths to feed — his girlfriend, Maria, Missy's assistant, was pregnant with his child. No one knew, even Geraldo, Maria's father, and both Maria and Ricardo were suddenly faced with some major life decisions.

Ricardo kept walking, hands in pockets, hood up on his coat. His options continued to rotate, over and over until he knew what he and Maria needed to do before it was too late.

§

Mellissa enjoyed the Weather Station's quiet atmosphere. Her work seemed to go faster when she worked the night shift, 6 p.m. to 2 a.m., as she did this particularly cold starry night. Normally, she and Rod would work the shift together, but Rod decided to take some time off during the holidays.

Bridgett filled in for Rod and Sonny extended his own hours because he always had additional paperwork to do. It was just the three of them on duty. Mellissa sat at her desk going over the latest weather forecast with Bridgett. "It looks as if the atmospheric river coming our way is being pushed by a more complex weather pattern. It's… it's as if there's a series of atmospheric rivers right behind it… less than 12 hours behind." Bridgett had been half listening at first, but Mellissa's tone had a sense of urgency that caused Bridgett to swivel in her chair and lean in closer. "Trade me sides, I need to see that," Bridgett whispered as she enlarged the screen on the monitor. "Umph, yeah, okay, I see what you mean, Mellissa. Good catch. Don't send that forecast out yet. I'll get back with you, I need to talk to Sonny." A few minutes later, Mellissa could hear the two of them discussing the situation.

The weather forecast from the Moses Lake station had to be changed from a weather update to a Weather Storm Warning, not unusual for December, but the magnitude of the change could be viewed as a major mistake by the MLWS for not seeing it before. As a result, Mellissa carefully worded the Warning so as not to cause any unnecessary problems, but to alert people to be ready for snow IN ABOVE AVERAGE AMOUNTS.

Normally, a forecast this time of year would rely on past snow levels to aid in the forecast, but the structure of the weather systems building up north were so complicated they appeared to be above normal by Bridgett and Sonny. After a short meeting with Sonny, and a phone call to national headquarters, a forecast was finally approved.

Mellissa's carefully crafted third draft would go out on time at 2 a.m.

Area Forecast
Issued December 18 @ 0200 by MLWS
Moses Lake, WA

Alert. Winter Storm Warning!
Issued 2 am for all 8 Central Washington
Counties: Benton, Chelan, Douglas, Grant,
Kittitas, Klickitat, Okanogan and Yakima.

Today through the weekend temperatures decreasing rapidly to 27 degrees high and 19 low through Sunday evening. Snow levels between 6–8 inches at 2000 feet, 18 inches to 3 feet above 4000 feet. Winter weather to be expected for the next two weeks bringing icy road conditions and drifting snow. Stay tuned for updates as conditions may prove to be extreme in the long range forecast.

Mellissa sat back after pushing the *save* button on her computer. Her area forecast would reach all media outlets in time for early morning broadcasts, including the internet, and six local newspaper publications in: Moses Lake, Yakima, Wenatchee, Tri-Cities, Othello, and Omak.

Sonny asked both Mellissa and Bridgett to work late in order to keep an eye on the unusual weather conditions. "I need my most trusted and professional forecasters on this," Sonny declared with a wink and a smile before donning his coat and hat and leaving for the Grant County Airport to meet with their weather team who called a special meeting.

All of a sudden, and for the first time, Mellissa questioned her ability to manage the weather conditions they faced. She had no problem dealing with normal day-to-day situations that historically occurred and were taught at the university, but her intuition had her doubting herself as she watched the storm systems converge on the huge wall monitor. She and Bridgett decided to order out and have DoorDash deliver. No one would be leaving anytime soon.

§

Missy and Maria were in the middle of taking inventory in the tack room. Missy, on a ladder, asked Maria to hand her a box of brushes used for grooming the horses. Maria put her clipboard down and bent down to lift the box when she stopped suddenly, dropping the box. Missy nearly fell off the ladder before making her way over to where Maria stood. "What's the matter, Maria?" Maria had rolled backward onto her bum and needed help up. "Oh, I'm…I'm just clumsy, sorry." Maria took one step and had to get off her feet fast. "Maria? What's going on?"

Missy knew something else was happening because of the way Maria held the sides of her stomach. "Are… are you pregnant?" Maria burst into tears as Missy held her close. Maria had been wearing loose fitting clothes lately, causing Missy to wonder. "I didn't want you or my father to know. Ricardo and I have been discussing what to do next. I didn't know how to tell you…or my father." Missy nodded, but knew she had to be careful about how to respond to her dear friend. Missy understood, full well, what Geraldo might do to Ricardo if he found out. "You're going to be fine. Everything is going to be fine, Maria. Missy stood and looked out the window toward the barn. She had an idea. "As I see it, Maria, you have two choices; You can go to your father, today, and explain your situation and your plans with Ricardo. You do have a plan, Maria, right?" Maria sat shaking her head. "Or you could contact Planned Parenthood."

They held hands as Maria briefly explained that her pregnancy was, surprisingly, in the third trimester. She had been in contact with a local OB, which had made life difficult for her the last few months. She and Ricardo hadn't had time to plan. Missy pulled Maria close and reassured her that she was not to worry. They headed to the ranch house and spent the next two hours working on what needed to happen — immediately — starting with Ricardo.

Chapter 12

Michael sat wiping off sweat after his workout at the VA Center. His trainer and fellow veteran, Goliath, had just finished putting him through the paces of a new routine that worked his hip flexors and lower back.

The government had come through with the funds for a new prosthesis for his amputated leg and Goliath wanted to make sure Michael was physically fit to use the new titanium model. Michael held his hands up in the shape of a "T" signaling timeout. "Drink some water. How do you feel, Mike?" Goliath stood over his friend knowing that Michael could feel every muscle and tendon left in his body. Michael looked up with hands held high and replied, "You are the most cruel person I know." Goliath pulled his friend up into a standing position. Michael stood bouncing on one leg as he reached for the side wall of the gym to steady himself. Goliath had a look of complete surprise at Michael's remark regarding his teaching style, before breaking out in a deep roar of laughter. Michael shook his head as he attached his new leg and added, "I do feel stronger. I didn't know I was so out of shape." Goliath patted him on the shoulder as Michael headed to the showers. Goliath reached out and stopped him. "You had something you wanted to tell me, something beyond my being a cruel taskmaster." Michael looked at him and nodded. Michael suggested they grab a coffee at the place next door, Deep Breath Latte, after his shower — he did have something to discuss regarding his brother, Chet.

Goliath had recruited a couple of gym members to help decorate the entrance to the place. While Michael showered, Goliath hurried to his office and grabbed his Santa hat and jingle bell necklace before helping to hang Christmas lights around the workout studio. With the big day a few weeks away, he wanted the mostly concrete block walls to join in the celebration for Santa and the New Year. "The Santa hat is a good look for you, big guy." The two women weightlifters who were helping hang the lights appreciated Goliath's height as he assisted in the decorating. He was the only one who didn't require a ladder in order to place four large wreaths as his helpers completed hooking all the lights up and around the gym. A perfectly shaped six-foot Douglas Fir was beautifully decorated by Goliath's yoga instructor and one of her students. They were in the midst of cleaning up as Michael and Goliath walked past on their way out. "Namaste, and Merry Christmas," both Michael and Goliath shared in unison.

The two veterans walked next door to Deep Breath and ordered 20 ounce breves with no flavor, egg bites, and two fruit plates. The owner, a student of Goliath's evening class for ladies only, knew to fill the fruit bowls with extra helpings. "Thanks, Dawn, you're the best," Goliath said as he and Michael watched her serve them in the corner booth. The tall blonde, with an attractive muscular build, winked as she walked off. Goliath took a first sip of his breve as he watched Dawn walk away. "I would take a bullet for that lady," Goliath said as he placed a load of fruit on Michael's plate. "So, what's on your mind, Mike?"

Michael tried to speak with a mouth full of egg and gestured with his plastic fork to wait a second. Once he could talk, Michael explained how his brother Chet had shared a concern about a fieldworker on the Hawthorne Ranch. Evidently, a new man, named Enrique, was causing problems for Missy, and Chet wanted some *big brother* advice. "What's this Enrique doing?" Goliath asked as he took a quick sip of water, trying to cool down the hot egg bite.

Michael spent the next few minutes relaying what Missy had told Chet about Enrique. She felt her father was pressured into hiring the guy by Geraldo, a trusted employee. "We don't usually hire people this time of year, but Geraldo was insistent, which wasn't like him." There was something about owing a favor to an old friend, so her father agreed and two days later the man showed up. Since then, life at the ranch went from a smooth running operation to workers complaining about Enrique's behavior — he even caused two fights in the bunkhouse. One of their best workers, Ricardo, told Missy that Enrique was not to be trusted. She added that Ricardo, one of their best and brightest workers, and Maria, her assistant, were having a baby. And Enrique's presence just added to the drama. In addition, one of the field hands, while checking fences recently, reported one of their workers was on an ATV running through a pasture at high speed. Chet told Michael that he saw Enrique parking an ATV late one night, which was unusual for him to be out roaming around at that time. Missy told Chet she feared they'd made a big mistake hiring Enrique and that something mysterious was going on.

Goliath looked at Michael, took a sip of his latte and said, "I think someone needs to talk to this Enrique person." Goliath offered his help. "Thanks, I'll let you know. Chet sounded desperate," Michael responded with a head nod.

They left together, Michael headed to work and Goliath to his studio office. A few of Goliath's military veteran weightlifting students passed Michael in the parking lot as he made his way to his Company pickup. He'd put in enough time at the Magic Trucking Company, in the past few weeks, that Peter decided it was time Michael felt more included in the business. He called Michael into the office last week and asked how his rehab was going. Michael explained that he'd passed all his tests, even his driving test, which enabled him to drive a car or truck with automatic drive. "That's good news," Peter said as he handed him the keys to a company pickup. What Michael didn't know is that his sister, Cindy, who had been keeping an eye on Michael's rehabilitation progress through a friend at the hospital's rehabilitation center, had already called Peter with the good news about Michael's progress.

When Michael first sat in the truck's driver seat he hesitated before turning the key over. There was a sudden realization as to how far he had come since his return from overseas. He told himself that by turning the key in the ignition he was officially moving on with his life. He smiled about that memory as he drove away from the VA workout center.

§

Enrique met, as ordered, with two men he didn't know at the Apple Inn, a roadside diner on the highway on the outskirts of Yakima. They were part of a new branch of an old criminal organization that would be distributing only Fentanyl in the region. "Where are the drugs now?" The smaller of the two, a white man with a white goatee, a sharp pointed nose, and beady dark eyes, identified as Mister Z, whispered in a low scruffy voice. The man made Enrique nervous, as did his sidekick, a much larger man with metal in his teeth and wearing orange tennis shoes. Enrique didn't realize he'd be connecting with — a white man. A small voice inside him said to beware. Mister Z checked his cell phone while the big guy chewed on a toothpick playing stare down with Enrique. When it was his turn to talk, Enrique went ahead and told them that he had the drugs at the Hawthorne ranch. Mister Z looked up at his partner, winked, and slowly explained Enrique's role in the operation as the captain of the distribution center, which now became the Hawthorne ranch. Enrique swallowed hard with the thought that the ranch now had a new designation. Z noticed Enrique's hesitation and asked if there was a problem. It took Enrique a few minutes and some fast talking to reassure the men of his loyalty. Z smiled as he reached over and pinched Enrique's good side of his face. Z then outlined what Enrique needed in order to be prepared for more drops to arrive beginning the first of the year. "The first drop was a test and you passed it." Enrique let a long breath out. Mister Z went on to explain that it was Enrique's responsibility to find a place on the ranch, to store the contraband safely. Enrique came to America not knowing the part he would play, he just wanted to make money and retire young and wealthy like every American. The conversation ended with the fact that any loss of product or interruption in the distribution of product would come back on Enrique — "And you don't want that to happen, believe me a-migo." The little man got up, pushed the much bigger man toward the door, saluted Enrique with a gloved hand, and as he left, whispered, "We'll be in touch."

It began to snow as Ricardo pulled up outside the Apple Inn. Enrique came out the front door as if he was looking for a fight. Ricardo had been in Yakima picking up ranch supplies and was on his way to pick up Enrique when he received a call that the meeting had ended. Enrique slapped Ricardo on the leg after entering the truck. "Well…it's all set." Ricardo remained stoic as he turned on the blinker and entered the highway, shifting as the truck gained speed. He had to be careful, the snow had begun to stick and the truck slid slightly as he hit third gear. "What's all set?" Ricardo still hadn't given Enrique his answer about helping out with the drug distribution. His answer would be no, but Ricardo didn't know how to tell Enrique. What he did know was that his answer had to happen soon, because he and Maria were planning on leaving before Geraldo found out about the baby. "We, you and I, mi amigo," Enrique answered, "are going to be rich." As Enrique went into how the Fentanyl would be distributed, Ricardo stopped listening and concentrated on the swirl of snowflakes that were beginning to make it difficult to see.

§

Mellissa's cell phone rang causing her to blink her eyes open. Her clock read four in the afternoon. It didn't make sense until she realized she and Bridgett had worked late on the night shift. Mellissa remembered getting to bed sometime around six in the morning. "Yes, I'm here. Bridgett?" Her colleague called because two people reported being sick and wouldn't make it to work, plus Rod was still on his holiday vacation. "I hate to do this to you, but I'm out of options." Before Mellissa could answer, Bridgett continued. " Besides, Mellissa, you need to see what's happening with this new storm front." Mellissa quickly dressed and made her way to the station. As she stepped out into the new snow, about ten inches, she noticed her socks were two different colors. "Great."

Sonny was out shoveling snow away from the front steps of the weather station as she pulled up in front. The station manager stopped shoveling as she walked up. "Back so soon?" Sonny always had a way of making people laugh. But the look on his face told her something was wrong. "Bridgett's waiting for you, I'll be right in, we have a problem." Sonny looked as though he hadn't been home, which means he's been on duty for at least 24 hours.

As Mellissa made her way to her desk, Bridgett stopped her midway, laptop in hand. "Check this out." She showed Mellissa a series of dark masses coming in three phases from the north, beginning at the north pole. "It looks like someone spilled ink on the screen." Bridgett couldn't hold the computer still, so they went to the larger weather screens at the end of the room. When Mellissa enlarged the weather image on the screen, seven feet wide, they both dropped back. "Oh my God! What is that?" Mellissa shouted. Sonny came up from behind them stamping off his feet and warming his hands. "I've never seen that much synoptic atmospheric activity, period," Sonny offered as he slowed to a stop with his mouth open. Mellissa wondered if they were looking at history in the making. Sonny suggested that they'd have to consider weather patterns that pre-dated anything in the current data base. "We can't just stand here, we have to send a revision out immediately!" Sonny sounded as if he was a military general and they were going to war.

Mellissa sent a text out to her family, everyone, telling them to watch the news for updates and to be ready for heavy snow conditions. "DON'T CALL ME RIGHT NOW. I'LL GET BACK WITH YOU SOON."

§

Holiday mornings on the Hawthorne Ranch were especially warm and comforting for Missy as she sat with her father going over the weekly work schedule. She glanced out the kitchen windows and took a quick sip of tea. The view had changed dramatically since yesterday morning. White frost could be seen over most of the landscape as the sun rose, attempting to erase the icy whiteness. Her father also took a break and crossed under the hanging copper pans to refill his coffee. Missy could see a worried look on the face of the man she loved and admired most in life. That look was new for him and it concerned her. Missy kept the cup close to her face as her father returned to his kitchen island bar stool. She lowered the cup and asked, "What is it, father?" He just smiled and adjusted himself in his seat.

Since most of the workers had been sent home to Mexico after wrapping up their seasonal work, the schedule changed. All of the cattle had been relocated or sold, which left the sheep and horses to be cared for by Geraldo, Maria, Ricardo, and Enrique. Missy knew the reworking of the schedule wasn't what bothered her father. Maybe something to do with her brother? Finally, Jake looked at his daughter and said, "When I asked Geraldo why Enrique needed to stay, he hesitated. That's not like him. It was as if Geraldo had something to hide." Jake Hawthorne expected his employees to be open and honest with him. He never doubted Geraldo, until now.

Since her father's return from taking Tim to rehab in Arizona, he seemed anxious, which was not like her father. Missy found herself having to choose whether to unload her concerns or hold them back and deal with them herself. In that moment she made the decision to tell her father everything or else face the possibility of consequences later. Missy looked away then back at her father, knowing what she had to share about Maria and Ricardo, in addition to her distrust for Enrique, could change who they employed in the future and possibly more. Just as she was about to speak, her phone rang. She looked at the caller ID and excused herself and walked into the hallway. "Chet. I'm with my father right now… what? Enrique? When? Oh, okay. Call when you're close." Missy walked back into the kitchen. "Father, we have to talk."

§

MLWS
Weather Emergency Update!
For Immediate release – Attention: All 8
counties in Central Washington

Expect blowing snow and icy road conditions
for the next 48 to 72 hours. Temperatures
steady at 25 high / 15 low Wind 25 mph
with gusts up to 40 mph out of the north by
northwest for the next 72 hours. Emergency
Responders expect Blizzard Conditions – take
appropriate actions. Snow levels are expected
to reach one to two feet in the valley with
drifting snow. Expect I-90 to be monitored
for closure in the next 24 hours. All citizens
are encouraged to remain in place in order
to reduce unnecessary travel and provide
emergency responders complete road access
when necessary. If you must go outside, dress
for extreme weather – sub zero conditions to
-10 degrees in overnight hours due to high
winds.

Mellissa called her mother after sending the weather release.
" Oh, hi, sweetie," "Mom, listen. There's a storm." "What?
Wait, I'll get your father." "No. Stop. I'm calling to let you and
Pops know that the incoming snow storm has the potential to
be the worst we've ever seen in this area. You have to prepare
yourselves."

"Oh, dear, are you okay there at the station? You guys are
out in the middle of nowhere!" Mellissa put her hand over the
phone, took a deep breath, let it out slowly, and assured her
mother that they would be fine at the station. Mellissa's main

concern focused on family and the community that needed to understand what was happening and to take appropriate action. "Maybe Cindy should come and stay with you two. What do you think, Mom?"

Maggie promised to call Cindy as soon as they hung up. The next person on Mellissa's list was Peter. She called to give him the same warning, which he was only too happy to receive. "Thanks, Sis, I'll begin shutting things down now," was Peter's response. Before he signed off he told her that Chet was out on a delivery with one of the older model trucks — they were that busy. "I know he planned to stop by the Hawthorne Ranch before returning this afternoon. I'll find him."

What Peter didn't know was that Michael and Goliath planned to meet Chet at the Hawthorne Ranch. Missy called Chet earlier and told him that Maria and Ricardo were missing. She suspected Enrique had something to do with it, even though Maria's pregnancy would have been enough for them to take off together. Geraldo had been too busy with the horses and still did not have any clue as to Maria's condition. Even though she was in her third trimester, she did a good job of covering up her baby bump. Ricardo had the use of the old Chevy truck used to haul feed out to the pastures. The truck was purchased used when Missy's father and mother started the ranch nearly 25 years ago. Missy could only hope that the two of them were okay, especially with the new snow storm beginning to howl.

When Chet turned off I-90 he needed to put chains on the truck in order to drive on the side roads. He promised himself he'd make the chains happen at the ranch. He hadn't driven *Old Reliable* since the first day he met Missy. Although the front end problems had been fixed, Chet had his doubts about how well the truck would handle in a blizzard. The storm had most drivers staying home and off the highway. Those that dared to drive had two choices: slow down or head for the ditch. Chet decided to trust the old ride, and his instincts, as he headed to the ranch.

§

A Seattle-based climate change watchdog group posted a message on their Facebook account once Mellissa's Weather Alert was posted on the internet:

> Mother Nature has had it. The time had come
> to send a message.
>
> *Blow and blow harder my wind. Bring the darkness*
> *that will serve to let them know that there's no stopping*
> *this frozen flake messenger hidden in this mysterious*
> *seasonal flow. Wake up you sleepy people, the time for*
> *action has come, and will continue until you take notice*
> *of what you all have done.*

§

Missy heard Chet's truck pull up close to the barn and went to the ranch house window. She watched Geraldo open the large sliding doors as Chet jumped down from the MTC delivery truck. "We didn't schedule a delivery today, Chet," Missy shouted as she came running up and greeted Chet with a big hug. "I'm glad you're here. Thank you. Don't say anything, Geraldo doesn't know about Maria," she whispered in Chet's ear. Chet nodded his understanding to her as he turned and waved at Geraldo who had slid the last door open. "Geraldo, thanks, I need to chain up the truck, mind if I pull it in further?" The man nodded his head and waved him in then helped with the chain up.

Just as they finished, headlights appeared coming down the road leading to the front gate. "That has to be Michael, he's my back up." Missy looked at Geraldo, who had a quizzical look on his face. "Back up?" Geraldo said as he watched Missy push the gate control box, on the side of the barn, opening the big iron gate. Missy walked over to Geraldo and quietly asked, "Do you have a minute?." She, as carefully as she could, explained Maria's pregnancy and disappearance with Ricardo, questions about Enrique, and that Chet and Michael were willing to help if there was any trouble. In the meantime, Michael drove up. Geraldo sat on a bale of hay with his head in his hands. Missy patted his back and whispered as she turned to greet Michael. "I'll be back."

Chet was relieved to see Michael. His big brother had no problem walking in the snow that was nearing a foot deep. He greeted Chet and Missy as he made his way around the truck. "Hey, Chet, Missy, we're here to help." Missy met Michael with a warm hug, not expecting anyone else. "Surprise." Goliath shook off the snow and pulled up the hood on his full-length winter coat as he leaned over to give Missy a hug. They'd met at the Bellman's Christmas dinner and she still couldn't believe the size of the man. Without looking, Missy said, "I want you guys to meet someone." Missy meant to introduce Michael and Goliath to Geraldo, but he was gone. She knew where he might be. "We have to hurry."

§

Enrique enjoyed the solitude of the bunkhouse with the others gone. Their absence also allowed for the preparation of separating the large bag of Fentanyl pills into smaller bags for sale. He had to be ready for local distribution by January first, which was fast approaching. Enrique had to be ready or else.

The air drop provided him with 10,000 pills, 20 clear plastic bags of 500 each. Enrique looked out the main window of the bunkhouse, checking the courtyard one more time. He knew that Geraldo had no reason to come to the bunkhouse so he locked and bolted both entry doors.

Enrique inner-locked his figures together and stretched his arms out forward in preparation of what he was about to do. He pulled one of the plastic bags from the black canvas cargo bag and opened it on an old wooden table below the window with the shade drawn. He had several smaller "Sale Bags" ready to fill. As he separated out ten pills for the first bag, he imagined how rich he was going to be a year from now. He had mixed feelings about using the ranch as the center for distribution. But, the Hawthorne Ranch was the perfect location, no one suspected anything like drug distribution happening here. His mind went crazy with possibilities — and the consequences. Maybe someday he would buy the ranch from the Hawthornes, clearing his conscience as he thought about becoming a rancher.

He pulled the shade back slightly to check as the snow kept coming. *Nerves*. Enrique set the bunkhouse radio to a local station that played Latin music, which helped fill the void as he counted and sang along with a few of the songs. One of his favorites came on and his singing volume picked up to the point he didn't hear the rush of footsteps that came fast toward the bunkhouse front door. Geraldo tried to open the door, but it was locked. *Why?*

Suddenly, the solid wooden door crashed open and there stood Geraldo. "I knew you were up to no good, you bastardo!" Geraldo launched himself at Enrique. Pills went flying. Enrique knew he had locked the door, but the old man must have kicked it in. It was too late to hide. Geraldo had both hands around Enrique's neck. "Where is my daughter? What have you done with her?" Enrique didn't know where Maria had gone — he had to think fast. Enrique choked out a response, "Maria is missing?"

Geraldo danced Enrique backwards and up against the wall, spitting his words as he pushed tighter. "I'm going to kill you if you don't tell me what's going on!" Enrique hit Geraldo, hard, on the side of the head. Geraldo hit the floor and Enrique ran for the table. Enrique did his best to push the larger pill bag into the canvas bag that lay on the floor. "I'm sure they are fine, amigo. Take a moment and let me talk." Geraldo pulled himself up on all fours, saw what Enrique was doing with the pills and stood. His only thought was for Maria's whereabouts as he rushed toward Enrique. The new ranch worker turned drug dealer grabbed the canvas bag and held it in his chest. "I don't care about those," Geraldo shouted as he pointed to pills scattered on the table. "I want my daughter." And with that last statement he lunged for the taller Mexican for the second time. They both went to the floor with Enrique clutching a fist full of Fentanyl pills. Geraldo hit Enrique repeatedly until the pills came loose and a counter kick hit Geraldo square in the stomach. The blow sent Geraldo back as the front door fell open again. Enrique fumbled around inside the side pocket of his canvas bag and found his 12" knife. The knife had been given to him by Mr. Z. The little man with the beady eyes and terrible breath, told Enrique, "The knife is yours to keep with one condition — you have to use it." The sharpened blade of polished steel fit perfectly in a brass and leather ribbed handle. A brown leather sheath protected the knife's blade. The knife made Enrique feel respected.

He held the knife to Geraldo's throat as Missy pushed her way past Chet running toward the man holding the knife. "Don't you dare, Enrique or whoever you are." Time froze while all parties looked at one another. Enrique spoke first, "I won't harm him if you stand out of the way, I, we, need to leave."

Enrique felt a surge of energy as he stood with the tip of the knife touching Geraldo's neck, ready to exit. No one moved as Enrique, a head taller than Geraldo, pulled Geraldo backwards toward the open door. Just then a dark shadow appeared in the doorway. It was a person, the largest human Enrique had ever seen. "Hey there, Enrique. I'm Goliath and I'm here to break both of your arms and shove that knife up your holiday ass, unless of course, you let the man go and do as the young lady says." Goliath made his way across the room as he spoke. Missy moved so Goliath could get passed. The dark shadow advancing as Enrique attempted to close his mouth and make a run for it. "Comprender there, amigo?"

It seemed to Missy, and now Chet and Michael who had joined the room, that the man holding the knife had just pissed himself as he dropped the knife. "I…I wouldn't…ah, please. You, ah you asked about Maria and Ricardo…I saw them. I can help you. They left not long ago, they took the old ranch truck and headed west on Highway 2." Goliath smelled a rat and reached over, pulling the man a few inches off the ground and into his chest as if he were a rag doll. Enrique had a very worried look on his face as he pleaded for mercy, but stopped talking as Goliath placed a forefinger on Enrique's lips. "That's a good boy, now… go to sleep." Goliath punched Enrique once into a dreamstate and set him off to the side. Michael and Chet helped Geraldo to a bench seat nearby as Missy announced that she was calling the sheriff. "Ah, Missy, you might want to wait on that call," Michael and Goliath both suggested at the same time. "Tell her," Michael said to Goliath. "Missy, we need to talk to this piece of…ah…dirt, before the cops. Besides, no one is moving too fast with that storm coming." Michael added, "You can call the authorities as soon as we find out a little more about this Fentanyl laying around here. "Fentanyl?" The room said in unison, including Geraldo. "Yep. Fentanyl is causing our veterans problems and I'm part of a task force dedicated to prevention and rehabilitation. I can't tell you any more about my role in this, but let's just say that I know people who would be very interested in what's going on here," Goliath said in an authoritative manner.

Michael carried a full basin of water over to where Enrique lay passed out on the floor. He threw it in the man's face. The splash caused Enrique to come awake. "What? Oh, maldito sea." Time was ticking, Missy wanted to find Maria and Ricardo, and Goliath and Michael needed some answers. Enrique, feeling threatened, and new to the Fentanyl effort, was more than helpful with information, which allowed Missy to make the call and for Chet, Michael and Goliath to be on their way to look for Maria and Richardo.

Goliath sent a message to his drug enforcement contact with a photo of Enrique before they left the ranch. The giant of a man had a long history of dealing with illegal drugs going back to his first deployment in Afghanistan. His commanding officer picked him out of a crowd of soldiers, which was easy to do because of his height. Goliath was chosen to serve on a special drug task force. The Pentagon made it mandatory for all branches of the service to take action against drug use in the military. Some of the heaviest users were soldiers deployed overseas. Goliath quickly became one of the leaders on his task force. He took it upon himself to go out of his way to help those that had his back. As a result he had more success in finding and eradicating illegal drugs and the traffickers that made it possible. Sergeant Kenny Richards received military honors from his commanding officer and the Secretary of Defense for his efforts. Goliath continued to serve veterans of all branches of military service through a special arrangement with the U. S. Defense Department for his rehabilitation gym in Moses Lake.

Geraldo stood over Enrique, checking the ties that secured him to one of the main support pillars of the bunkhouse. Missy spoke up, "The sheriff is on his way." Geraldo agreed to watch over Enrique until the sheriff arrived. "I don't care how long they take, I got him," Geraldo stated. Missy headed to the house to be with her father and explain what had just happened. Missy was sure that her father would join Geraldo in watching his newest hire. Once they learned of Maria and Ricardo's exit and direction, Chet, Michael, and Goliath agreed to find them and bring them home. Chet promised to stay in contact with Missy as the three men drove out of the Hawthorne Ranch heading west on Highway 2.

Chapter 13

Adding chains helped the Old Reliable gain traction over the drifting snow and ice on the unplowed highway. Unnoticed by the men in the truck were the old weather-beaten vinyl letters that formed the company name along both sides of the old truck. Edges of the lettering were beginning to giveway to the relentless pounding of snow and wind against the boxy ride. The letters in the word Magic were beginning to flap, especially the letter "C." Inside the cab, the bench seat allowed for enough room across so that all three could sit comfortably side-by-side. Michael and Chet decided earlier in the truck yard that the big truck would have better traction and more room. As it turned out, they were carrying blankets, a large generator and six space heaters from a delivery that canceled earlier in the day. Chet had some bottled water and a few Power Bars that he kept in his backpack behind the driver's seat just in case. Michael made a mental note to tune the two-way radio to the police scanner frequency after calling into Peter at MTC.

"Peter, this is Michael, do you read? Over."

Loud static responded as if it had something to say. "Come on." Michael adjusted the frequency button and tried again.

After a few seconds the static became less irritating as a familiar voice responded, "Michael, where are you guys? Over.

"Hey, Pete, just left the Hawthorne Ranch. We're heading north to find highway 2. Our current position is about a mile south of I-90."

"Roger. What's your ETA?" There was a noticeable pause as Goliath went from looking out the side window to watching Michael scratch a three-day beard with the mic while Chet smiled a cough as he drove. Then, "Mike? Over."

"I hear you Pete. Ah, we aren't coming back yet, we're on the hunt for two people… I'll send you a text to explain. Over."

There was a short pause, static, then, "Ah, roger that, Mike. Be careful guys. Mellissa just sent out an update on the weather — it's bad — more sn… ow…com… gerous conditions," as the radio transmission broke up.

After signing off with his brother, Michael checked his phone and found Mellissa's MLWS weather update. "He's not kidding, guys. This weather system is a monster."

The fuel gauge showed less than a quarter tank. They needed to gas up if they were to continue their search. Chet knew just the place, Phil's Stop and Romp, on the other side of I-90 in Ellensburg. Ten miles later the guys took turns going to the restroom and manning the fill up. The clock was ticking in regard to finding Maria and Ricardo — as the snow just kept coming. "Hi, Chet. You boys ought to think twice about making any deliveries today," said Phyllis, a tall slender gray-haired woman in her 60's standing at the register. She added that she planned to close up within the hour as darkness had finally taken over the snowy sky. "I hate to close early, three days before Christmas. Normally, this is a busy time for us." The attractive owner of the mini truck stop visited with Chet and made a joke about Goliath being able to push if they ever ran off the road. She looked the giant up and down, loosening the ties on her sweater as she did. "Is it hot in here all of a sudden, or is it just me?" Phyllis whispered to herself. The last customers were leaving as Goliath blew her a kiss as he raced out to join Chet and Michael. Chet put the truck in first gear as Goliath closed and locked the passenger door. He checked the driver's side view mirror in time to see the neon sign and interior lights being turned off around Phil's station.

§

Cindy returned Mellissa's call and assured her that all was well on the Bellman front. "Where are the guys?" she added. "Call Peter, he said he'd be tracking Chet's truck. I believe Michael is with him." Cindy hung up and let Maggie know that there would be just the three of them for dinner.

Mellissa sat alone in the weather station, which was highly unusual. Two people who had requested transfers were now working in Spokane, two others were home sick, and Rod was out until the first of the year. Bridgett had to go home to check on her family and fix dinner before returning. She had been at the station most of the last three days and her husband, a good guy who never complained, was beginning to worry about his wife's health. "I'll be back by six tonight," Bridgett's parting comments as she made her way to her car. Mellissa smiled and took a deep breath. She was sending out the latest weather forecast that Bridgett had just approved.

Sonny had to pick up his wife who couldn't start her car at the school where she worked. He wanted to take her home, shower before returning later, possibly around eight.

Just as Mellissa pushed "send" on the latest forecast she noticed a surge in the atmospheric river that suddenly gained in intensity. "That's really odd," Mellissa whispered to herself. She had a sudden chill and reached for her holiday sweater hanging on the back of the chair. A huge, green colored mass began to form on the large wall monitor. The snake-like activity appeared to be taking over the screen as it slithered slowly from the Arctic around the top of Alaska heading toward coastal western Canada.

The larger of the three screens at the end of the room started to pixelate, the lights throughout the station began to flicker, a moment later everything went black. Mellissa took a deep breath and on the exhale she reached for her phone, swiped up and accessed her flashlight. She was thankful her phone was fully charged because next, she went outside and fired-up the generator. Sonny had shown her how to run the generator last Fall when a thunderstorm knocked out the power. She turned off most of the lights in the room except for those around her kiosk. The screens up front came back on along with two space heaters that were now facing her desk. The office temperature was a cool 65 degrees. Both Bridgett and Sonny called to say they were unable to make it back, but would try as soon as power was restored and the roads were clear.

Mellissa decided to make a call — to Rod Lingo.

§

Maggie carefully finished rehanging the bubble lights on the lower half of the tree. "Pops never seems to be able to set them straight. They have to be straight in order to… bubble." Cindy stood back and agreed that the tree looked perfect with her mother's added touch. The addition of the bubble lights, especially in working order, reminded Cindy of past Christmases, warm and safe.

Maggie let out a satisfying breath and went to the bookshelf that contained old record LP's in addition to hard bound books. Maggie stood, carefully reviewing the records until she found the Christmas section. She turned to Pops and pulled out an old favorite Christmas album by Bing Crosby. "This man knew how to sing, isn't that so, Bruce?" Pops seemed distracted and didn't answer as he walked. Instead, he made a comment about how much Maggie continued to fuss with the tree. "I'm headed outside to clear the driveway, one more time, in case Mellissa stops by."

Cindy and her mother both looked at each other as Pops left out the back door. "He's worried about your sister." They both knew that snow removal would be the best exercise for Pops. Hopefully, it would clear his mind of worry and the driveway of snow. Pops had the reputation of being a worrier. Maggie remembered the times when the girls, especially Mellissa, started dating. He would begin pacing if they were five minutes past curfew. And woe be it to any young man who tested his rules. Maggie knew Pops had concerns for both girls, but that there was a special place in his heart for Mellissa. She also knew that Mellissa had her hands full at the weather station.

§

The old Hawthorne Ranch truck finally gained traction thanks to the help of two men who stopped to help Maria and Ricardo. It was the third time they'd needed assistance since leaving the ranch two hours earlier.

"How much further?" Maria had been having contractions, but she hesitated telling Ricardo. "If I can keep this old truck on the road for another two hours we should be in the Olsen's driveway. How are you and the little one doing?" Maria could feel another contraction coming on and couldn't hold it in any longer. She let out a loud shout as she leaned forward, hands on the dash. "Maria!" It was all Ricardo could do to keep the truck from going sideways. Ricardo reached over as he slowed to touch Maria's shoulder.

They were on their way to a small farm, further north past Wenatchee, where Ricardo had worked for an older couple. They were apple growers, but over the years, the owners had decided to reduce the size of their business and began selling off acres of their property until they had a more workable size, on ten acres, a barn, and their modest home. When Ricardo called to ask if he could stop by with a friend, they were very pleased. What he didn't tell them, primarily because he didn't know himself, was how long he and Maria would need to stay. Ricardo hoped to find work in the area, in the Spring.

Maria sat back in the seat, smiled at the father of their child, and assured him that she could wait two hours before they reached their destination. But she wasn't as confident about the little one.

§

The wipers were having a tough time keeping up with the heavy downpour of snow that just kept coming. "I'm not from around here, but it seems to me that this weather is becoming a big challenge," Goliath offered as Chet kept having to adjust the wiper speed.

"Hey, Chet, this is Peter, where are you guys? Over." Michael picked up the mic and responded, "Hey, Pete. We're out here playing in the snow. Over." The radio static lingered a few seconds before Peter replied, "Very funny, Mike. Didn't know you were riding along in order to have fun in the snow."

Michael gave Peter an update on weather and road conditions and that he, Chet, and his buddy Goliath were serious about locating Maria and Ricardo. Peter suggested that if they reached the Canadian border to turn around and head home. He reminded Michael that they were in the oldest truck in the fleet, and that the local authorities were dealing with a massive amount of emergencies, and may not be able to help.

"Road accidents are at an all time high and continue to keep responders extremely busy. The governor is considering calling for the National Guard to help. I-90 will be shut down soon around here. I'll be on my phone, keep in touch. Out."

Missy had mentioned to Chet that she overheard Ricardo say something about a farm north of Wenatchee. "I guess he worked there for a couple of years harvesting apples." So that's where they were headed.

Chet stayed on Highway 28 after making the turn in Quincy. The truck accelerated to a higher speed as it pushed its way out into the main flow of the small highway when Chet dropped it into third gear. Moments later flashing blue and red lights appeared, winking a warning through the curtain of falling snow. "State Patrol, Chet. Let's see what's going on," Michael stated as he put a hand on Chet's shoulder. Chet slowed as the three men saw something they each admitted later, they couldn't believe. About 50 yards ahead and off to the right of the road, a pile of snow revealed the tail end of a Greyhound bus sticking straight up, like a multi-colored croquet goal post. It looked as if the bus had been tossed by a giant and landed like a spoon in a bowl of sugar. People were standing along the other side of the road, including a Highway Patrol Officer. Chet put the truck in neutral, set the brake and kept the engine running as all three exited.

The officer that approached them had the appearance of a snowman, covered from head to toe with the white stuff. "Hey, boys, who let you out, today?" The officer, a female about six foot two with a deep voice, came forward holding a large flashlight. She wore official knit headgear instead of the Smokey the Bear brimmed hat. With the storm, it had been dark for about a half an hour and it was freezing cold. Her face looked frozen as she attempted to say, "Where'd you find this big one?" Referring to Goliath. She turned toward the scene of the accident then turned back. "We could use some help getting the driver out of the bus."

The bus was empty, except for the driver. "He was on his way to pick up riders who'd been stranded in Wenatchee for the last six hours. Their bus had broken down near Lake Chelan and had to be towed to the depot in Wenatchee." The more she talked, the harder it was for her to express herself. She identified herself as Officer Davis and added, "We need more rope for a rescue, any chance..." Chet had 200 feet of heavy duty vinyl rope in the truck and ran to get it. In the meantime, Officer Davis went to her cruiser to towel off her face and warm up.

Fifteen minutes later, Chet, Michael, and Goliath followed Officer Davis to the bus where two other men, both big, were standing. They had just closed a nearby gas station when the accident happened. One man held a rope, the other blew into gloved hands as they stood by a back exit door of the bus.

The Greyhound Express laid perfectly straight along the slope with the front embedded into a large snowbank that covered the windows halfway up from the front. "I'm pretty sure this guy," referring to the driver, "is out of the running for Greyhound's Driver of the Year Award." The men all laughed as Davis continued, "We need someone to take that rope down the aisle, hook it to this harness around the driver. Davis held the black and silver harness out for the guys to see. Once it's in place we pull the driver up and out so I can give him a ticket for driving too fast in poor weather conditions."

The officer sounded more like a teacher preparing to send a student to the principal's office rather than a passionate rescuer. Goliath looked at the woman and wondered if she'd ever been in the military. He was also curious to know if she was single.

Chet, after tying the two ropes together, volunteered to make the descent. Under the officer's direction, Chet, with one end of the rope tied around his waist, made his way down the row of seats, wondering to himself whether the bus would hold fast to the slope or break loose at any moment. About halfway down he tested that thought. He was using the armrests as footholds similar to descending a rockface, which was working just fine until he got going a little too fast and slipped, causing him to bang directly, and with some force, into the roof of the bus. Everyone up above froze as Chet swung back toward the floor of the bus. Davis ordered the men to pull on the rope, which tightened around Chet's waist, making him feel as though he'd just been gut punched, but slowed his swing. Chet found a new foothold and loosened the rope around his waist. He looked down at the older driver who appeared to be praying. "Sorry about that loud bang. Just hang on." The man tried to smile. Instead, nodded as he continued to hold on tight to the steering wheel.

The driver had a worried look on his face as Chet came down on top of the man, nearly knocking him over. "I think my ankle is broken," the man indicated by raising his leg slightly. He appeared to be middle aged and very cold, having spent nearly two hours waiting. Chet fastened the driver into the harness, then attached the rope. He waved to the officer who directed the men to "Pull!"

Once the driver was on his way up, Chet decided not to wait. He followed carefully behind, helping to guide the man as he retraced his steps.

The two made it to the top without incident. Trooper Davis didn't waste any time in escorting the driver to the back of the State Patrol cruiser. She wrapped the poor fella in a shiny silver rescue blanket while she said goodbye to the two men who helped pull during in the rescue. The three men who seemed to appear out of nowhere were ready to be on their way. Before they left, however, the officer tapped Chet on the shoulder and showed him the side of his truck and the company logo. "Those vinyl letters on your truck look like they're coming loose." Chet thanked her and made a mental note. As he turned toward the truck she patted him on the behind, thanked him, waved to the other two, and winked at the big black guy as she encouraged them to get off the road as soon as possible. Goliath said it sounded more like an order rather than a suggestion.

The old truck's heater struggled to keep them warm and the snow continued to challenge the wipers as they made their way down into the Wenatchee Valley where apples would be populating the surrounding trees in the Spring. For now, though, the landscape had the look of an Arctic glacier. Chet did his best to keep them on a highway that kept disappearing in the drifting snow.

They'd spent a good hour helping the officer, but decided to stop in Wenatchee anyway to eat and warm up before moving on.

§

Further north on the same highway, in the older model ranch pick up truck, Maria held tight to the dashboard as two more contractions came like lightning bolts, the last one creating some serious movement. "I'm close, Ricardo. I'm so sorry, Ricardo, I thought we had more time. How much further?" He could hardly stand to see Maria suffer as he struggled to find the edges of the highway. He questioned his insistence not to go to a hospital, but to get to the farm and have the baby there. He thought the hospital would have asked too many questions. Not that either Maria or Ricardo had anything to hide, but both were Green Card holders, which meant they may be subjected to some unknown rules violation. The U.S. Government was a benevolent watchdog in that respect — allowing them entry into the country, but under certain conditions that were always subject to change. Richardo knew that the Olsen's would be more than welcoming — and capable of helping.

Besides, Maria felt strong enough to have the baby naturally, like her mother and grandmother before her. Ricardo, on the other hand, was more reluctant as he faced parenthood. One thing for sure, he didn't want Maria to suffer, and trusted her instinct as they both agreed to keep going. His mind swirled 'round and 'round like the snowflakes coming and going as if teasing the truck's windshield. "Ricardo, look out!" His thoughts were suddenly interrupted as a mule deer and her fawn suddenly jumped out on the highway, directly in front of the truck. They were passing from a forested area, heading to the river on the opposite side of the highway. Within the chaotic blend of dark skies and driving snow, the truck's headlights mesmerized the two as they turned into statues. Richardo's first reaction was to hit the brakes on the icy road. In spite of the old truck's new all-season tires it began to spin. The front end gradually pulled away from hitting the deer and followed the back end around, once, twice, before ending up in an awaiting ditch close to the fast-flowing river. Maria screamed as the roadway disappeared and whiteness blew all around them until the truck became lodged, backwards, in a cushion of white. The impact was less than expected because of the heavy amount of snow that caught them like an outfielder on a baseball field. Maria felt nauseous, but thankful that they were alive and unhurt, including the baby who suddenly decided to take a break as the contractions lessened.

Ricardo unhooked his seatbelt and helped Maria sit more comfortably on the seat with her legs stretched out. Even though the contractions had paused, there was a new urgency called survival, facing them. The change in mood was thick as the truck began to cool with the truck engine off. Howling wind replaced the steady engine drone. The whistling, swirling forceful thrusts broadcast a threatening warning for them to beware and to hurry. The truck landed backwards in the ditch with the front end facing upward toward oncoming traffic. Not that anyone would notice the old Ford from the highway in the midst of the unrelenting snowfall.

"I have to find a way to get help," Ricardo whispered in her ear. Maria appeared to be resting comfortably with both hands on her stomach. She nodded after Ricardo kissed her gently on the forehead as he made his way across the seat. Maria settled into herself and prayed. She added a new prayer in addition to healthy birth and the safety of beloved Ricardo. The new prayer was for the storm to stop. "We can't make it without your help," Maria prayed.

When Ricardo passed the steering wheel, he had a thought. *Turn the headlights back on. Don't worry about the battery.* He reached over and pulled the knob. A sudden arch of light cascaded up like a searchlight at a Hollywood movie premiere. He rolled the driver side window down, thankful that it stood up above the snowpack, reducing the amount of snow falling inside as he made his way up and out. The last thing he heard as he left came from Maria — "*Amen.*"

§

An excerpt taken from:
The Wenatchee Herald – Editorial Page

The wind over the Cascades Mountains
continues to race toward the middle portion
of the State of Washington, in the form of
a wild and uncontrollable creature. Mother
Nature was definitely expressing herself today,
making a statement reinforcing the fact that
changes are happening to our climate. The
idea that four seasons could be counted on

and predicted with minimum irregularities
is currently being shattered, demolished and
replaced. *Nature was sick and tired of crumbling into
an unfixable morass. People of science are promoting
solutions and need to be recognized, let them take
charge. Governments of the world need to wise up or
we will all continue to suffer. Could this winter's storm
be a lesson and the exam will come later?*

For the first time in this newspaper's history,
we are unable to distribute today's edition
because of weather related problems.
Hopefully, our readers understand as we all
attempt to find our way in the coming days.

§

"Hey, Mellissa. I was just about to call you," Rod Lingo sounded genuinely concerned. Even though he was taking some time off from work, Rod continued to monitor the weather, especially since the two of them had discovered abnormal atmospheric patterns a few months ago. "You're on your own?" Mellissa assured him that she could ride out the storm, her concern was for the Moses Lake area and surrounding communities. "Rod, this storm shows no signs of slowing. I'm thinking we could get multiple feet of snow, up to eight feet in the central basin — that's unheard of!" Rod sensed that his normally level-headed friend was at her wits end. "I'm going to contact my uncle at the weather station in Alaska. They appear to be located near the source of the storm. I'll find out how things are there and get back to you, Mellissa." Rod had a sense of urgency in his voice. Mellissa thanked him and asked Rod to call as soon as possible, as her phone may run out of power. Any information from Alaska could be helpful in predicting future snow levels. She also wondered if the storm up north showed any signs of receding and asked Rod to thank his uncle. He said he would and to expect a call soon.

§

Chet, Michael and Goliath were on the road once again. Michael gave Officer Davis the two-way radio frequency for their truck along with his cell phone and asked that she contact them if she ran across Maria and Ricardo. Davis said she put out an All Points Bulletin on the truck and occupants, since the truck was reported "Missing" from the ranch. She promised to contact them with any update. Davis also encouraged the guys to be extra careful as they traveled north. "That part of the highway up there is dicey, even in good weather. No guard rails, more animals crossing the road, and fewer lighted areas. Good luck you handsome devils." The three searchers laughed about their time with the charming officer as they pressed on through deepening snow.

It was slow going in the 55 mph speed zone with the truck barely able to manage 40 mph. Michael and Goliath helped Chet spot road signs as they turned off Highway 28 and north on to Highway 285. They crossed the Wenatchee river and had just passed the town of Cashmere when the two-way static began rumbling.

Static…more static and then,"Michael Magic this is Officer Davis, do you read? Over." Michael reached for the mic and responded, "Hey, Davis, this is Michael — go ahead." The Officer described seeing a young man standing off to the side of the road waving a Mexican flag. "I thought, man that guy is tall until I slowed down and saw he was standing above the windshield of his truck."

Ricardo stood precariously on the hood of the truck. It was the third time he'd tried to flag someone down to help. His teeth were rattling beyond his attempt to stop them — he was so cold. He could hear Maria moaning in the cab below. Between his teeth rattling and the moaning he felt so helpless. *Wa…why did they come north?* They could have made a life in Mexico — maybe.

A beam of light coming through the snow storm snapped Ricardo out of his thoughts. He put the flag down and reached for the red towel Maria had given him. It meant less warmth for her, but she insisted on him waving the bright towel. "I saw something red flickering off to the right side of the road and slowed the cruiser." Trooper Davis couldn't believe her eyes. She could see some guy above the berm line at the side of the road. She said he slipped and fell when she slowed down. "It took me a few minutes, because of the deep snow, but I managed to find the top of the cab of an old truck. The poor fella was rubbing his head when I greeted him. Brother, was he relieved to see me." She confirmed that Ricardo ran off the road trying to avoid hitting a deer and fawn. The driver had no idea how long they'd been there. Ricardo appeared to be disoriented and had trouble remembering their situation, instead he turned and pointed at the passenger side window. "That's when he showed me the pregnant girl, Maria, and introduced himself. Ricardo was clearly shaken, and the young lady was about to become a mom. All I could think of was — Holy Jesus, we're going to have a baby right here in the snow bank."

Trooper Davis made several trips back and forth from her cruiser to the snow covered truck. On the last trip to her cruiser, she called in her location and retrieved a shovel. Davis received no response from headquarters, but didn't wait for confirmation. It took about thirty minutes, but the expecting parents were safely in the cruiser warming up. "You two huddle together under this all-weather warming blanket while I make another call. She changed the frequency on her radio, looked back at the young couple and pushed the call button. "This is Officer Davis calling my Magic buddies. Over." She proceeded to give Michael the directions to the scene of the accident, about five miles further on 285. "We're right behind you Davis — be there in 15. Out."

Goliath took a turn at driving the truck. Chet wore himself out trying to keep up with the mounting snow level and lay asleep with his head against the passenger window on a rolled up towel. Michael felt he could drive, if push came to shove, but decided not to risk it with his new limb. Goliath kept both hands on the steering wheel and poked Michael with his elbow as he said, "This truck reminds me of one we had in Afghanistan, remember, Mike? Michael looked forward as if searching the perimeter and slowly nodded.

Michael and Goliath had found an old Russian troop transport truck that had been abandoned by the Taliban. The truck had seen better years, but, after a few minutes spent under the hood, they had it running. Once they cleared the ride, Goliath's patrol, including Michael, used it as a decoy to fool the enemy into allowing them access into an opposing camp. What happened next earned the patrol medals for bravery and a severe reprimand from their commanding officer. "The only difference between the two trucks is that this one is much cleaner, drives a little better, and I don't think we're going to be yelled at when all of this is over," Goliath declared with a smile as they rolled up behind Officer Davis's cruiser and flashed their lights.

The storm continued to grow in intensity to the point that there was hardly any traffic on Highway 285. "I'm glad to see you guys. We are all going to be witnesses to a Christmastime birth, in the back seat of my cruiser, if we don't find the place Ricardo told me about, soon."

They decided to hustle and find the farm where Ricardo previously worked. "He says that the farm is just a couple of miles from here," Officer Davis smiled at Michael as she spoke to the group. "Let's vamoose before we can't move either your truck or my cruiser," Michael. Chet headed back to the truck repeating the word "vamoose" and chuckling to himself.

Officer Davis asked Goliath for a favor. Pointing to the young couple, Davis said, "Would you mind carrying Maria? She can't…" Before Davis could complete her request Goliath gently picked Maria up, introduced himself, and carefully trudged through the nearly two feet of snow that now covered the recently paved highway. The officer helped Ricardo, who appeared to be a little unsteady, probably because of his fall, follow the giant's trail to the cruiser. Officer Davis made her way around Goliath and opened a back door of the cruiser, laying out two blankets before Maria arrived. Davis thanked Goliath and watched as he walked away. Under her breath she whispered, "Now that's a man."

Goliath entered the truck just as Chet started the engine. Trooper Davis began to move out thanks to some shoveling Chet had done under the cruiser's front and back bumpers a few minutes earlier. The cruiser led the way with Richardo giving directions amidst Maria's crying out from contractions that were coming more frequently.

Chet was thankful for the rest he had now that he took another turn at driving. Michael called Peter on his cell phone, and Goliath worked on the truck's heater, which appeared to have a loose connection. "Hey, Pete. We've located Maria and Ricardo. Yes. They are safe, but she is very close to delivering the baby. Could you call Missy to let her know? Chet will call her soon as we find the farm we're trying to locate at the moment." Michael told Peter that the truck was going through three to four-foot drifts, and that they weren't sure when they'd be able to return. Peter asked that they keep in touch. "You three are in the midst of the worst winter storm to hit this region — get off the road as soon as you can!"

Officer Davis had experienced plenty of hard driving in the Army as a Military Transport Operator. She'd driven everything from troop carriers to missile launchers, munitions transports to Humvees. She'd requested a transfer to a tank operation, but the opportunity never developed. Corporal Davis blamed her commanding officer who seemed to think women were qualified up to a point. Instead, she accepted her promotion to Sergeant, which kept her from filing a complaint.

After two assignments overseas she returned home to Yakima, Washington with one year left to serve. She'd achieved an 88 status in the military, which is given to those who operate and or coordinate transport logistics. Unfortunately, when Linda Davis looked for her line of work in the private sector there weren't any suitable job openings. With the economy in decline she felt desperate until an Army recruiter/friend called about a job opening. He said that local law enforcement was looking for "People of Character" with military credentials. And as far as the recruiter was concerned, Linda fit the bill. She thanked the recruiter and once she received her honorable discharge, the former Sgt. Linda Davis applied.

Linda not only had experience in transportation, she also knew how to manage people, work on engines, take apart a gun and put it back together in record time. Sergeant Davis had skills that local law enforcement officials felt exceeded the expected from previous male and female applicants. The Washington State Patrol was more than pleased the day Linda Davis walked into the recruitment center.

Now, after serving the last two years on the job in Central Washington's four northern counties, Linda had been thinking about finding someone special and settling down. If that someone were to ask, Linda would describe herself as a feminine outdoorsy type with a flair for making the world a better place — or else. She had no siblings and was raised by her grandparents after her parents' deaths in an automobile accident when she was 16.

Officer Davis could feel the cruiser being tested as she drove through the fender-high drifts. "Ricardo, there's water in the door next to you, give Maria some. And hold on tight, we've got some curves in the road coming up." What Davis didn't say was that she had to remember where the road left off and the shoulder of the highway started, because the road was a solid white, running snakelike beside the Wenatchee River. It took all she could give, but they made it around the bend and headed straight along a fence line that came out of nowhere.

Close behind, the men in the Magic Trucking Company truck were equally thankful. Chet felt fortunate that the cruiser was leading the way. His thankfulness soon disappeared, however, with the tail lights of the cruiser. The snow had completely blocked his view forward. Even though he had driven this part of the county before, the river road was always a concern even in clear weather.

Chet slowed the truck and crept along wondering what to do if the truck began to slide sideways into a ditch or worse, the Wenatchee River. Suddenly, like a ball being tossed at the truck, a light appeared in the sky. It pierced the snow fall, became hazy then disappeared. Another dot of light appeared and became stronger. The beam of light came at regular intervals guiding the truck through a series of curves that serpentined along the river. Chet could feel the sweat begin to drip down his face. The other two in the cab were oblivious to what had just happened — lights appearing at just the right time. Michael, in the middle seat, had to place his hands on the dash in order to steady himself as the truck rode through and over the highway's uneven snow drifts.

The wind howled as if trying to express itself. Michael went into a quiet military mode, watching, surveilling, waiting, listening. Chet watched Michael through his peripheral vision while Michael searched. He worried about his big brother's reaction to what they were experiencing. Since coming back to the business, Michael had been doing well. Steady with his meds and therapy sessions treating his PTSD.

As they began to turn, a sudden gust of wind hit the truck broadside, causing the truck to make a sudden jerk to the right. Chet corrected his steering as the other two men hit him full force. Chet took the crushing blow well as he pushed back in an attempt to keep the truck upright as wind blew against the left side, nearly causing the truck to drop off on the right. Another correction was necessary while Michael and Goliath held fast to their positions by pushing on the dashboard, freeing Chet to steady the truck as it spun around 360 degrees on a particularly slick spot in the middle of the road, finally returning to where they had been heading. All three men looked at each other and burst out laughing. "You couldn't do that again if you tried little brother." Michael had the biggest smile on his face, which made Chet feel much better. All three felt more relaxed as they peered straight ahead. The dark sky continued to spit waves of snow at the windshield challenging the wipers to keep up.

Next to Michael, Goliath busied himself, again, by futzing with the heater, which had shown signs of working before the spinning incident. The fan stopped running due to the pounding of the truck against the roadway. At least that's what Goliath figured. Turns out he was right. "Heater, fixed," Goliath declared after a few twists and turns of his own with the wires. The cab was cool inside as Michael turned the switch and a familiar buzzing sound could be heard. "You're hired big guy," Michael said as he shifted in his seat and asked, "How's it going, Chet? Chet just smiled and nodded his head.

"F-fine."

A few moments later Goliath spoke again. "Hey where'd the cruiser go? Oh, wait, there, straight ahead. What's that?" Up ahead in the sky was a small bright white dot. "Can't be the sun. Must be a sign…or part of one," Chet offered. "Follow it," Michael added. Chet had to shift the truck into third gear in order to gain some speed. It didn't take long before the taillights of Davis's cruiser appeared. "Look, up ahead — it's them!" Goliath could hardly get the words out.

Man, I thought we'd lost them." Chet said as he smiled and looked over at Michael's friend with a big sigh of relief. "Yeah, me too!" Michael responded with a deep breath. All three men followed the pregnant couple expecting their first child under the star-like guide.

§

"There! That's it, over there." Ricardo pointed to a bright light shining through the snowy black sky. Officer Davis squinted her eyes and pulled herself forward in the driver's seat in order to get a better view. "Looks like a tiny flying saucer," declared Davis. "It's the Olsen's yard light, I'm sure of it," Ricardo assured her. Maria had to pull herself forward in order to see what they were talking about. "Oh, sure. I see…eeee, oweee," but had to lay back, distracted by another contraction.

Ricardo pointed to a partially covered road sign that read that slowly appeared as if it were floating past — Wells Road. The cruiser, followed by the Magic Trucking Company truck, made its way down Wells Road until they came to a slightly larger sign that read; Olsen Produce (closed). "Turn here."

Ricardo whispered as Maria appeared to be resting with eyes closed, still holding his hand with one of hers, the other on her stomach. Ricardo gently set Maria's hand down on the seat and called the Olsens on the phone to give them a heads up about the caravan about to enter their property. They had finally arrived.

Richardo shared what he knew about the Olsen's after Officer Davis asked. She had slowed the cruiser in order for the truck to catch up.

Sten Olsen and his wife, Georgia, both retired early from the healthcare industry to pursue their lifelong dream — create a working farm. Sten emigrated from Sweden to attend medical school at the University of Michigan where he met Georgia. Both shared the same goal of becoming a physician. It didn't take Sten long to shift his focus to major in hospital administration rather than becoming a doctor. As it turned out, he had more of a penchant for how business should run and not so much the human body.

Georgia decided to go ahead and attend medical school. In her second year, she became pregnant with their first and only child, a girl they named Luna. Sten actually suggested the name and gave anyone who asked the same explanation. "We met under a full moon and I asked Georgia to marry me under that same moon a year later. It just makes sense." Ricardo remembered Georgia nodding with tears coming down her face. Luna's middle name came from Georgia's mother's first name, Marie.

Georgia's priorities soon changed once she became a mother, devoting most of her time to their family, consequently, she reduced her academic hours and joyfully entered motherhood.

Her early medical training helped make the maternal leap, but the thought of becoming a doctor kept returning like a dreamy boomerang. And a few years later, after Sten graduated, Georgia had her degree and became a nurse practitioner.

She managed her own practice with two other practitioners and a PA, for nearly 20 years, until Luna graduated from high school and entered college at the University of Washington. Luna was currently in a Masters program in London studying to become an environmental scientist with a political science minor. As Luna worked to fulfill her dream, Sten and Georgia decided to go after theirs.

The Olsen's had been farming in the Wenatchee Valley for nearly four years and looked forward to creating a viable homestead. Ricardo had been their first farm hand and they considered him to be like a son. He worked hard and was a quick study when it came to farming. They were willing to help in any way they could, including allowing Ricardo, Maria and the baby to stay as long as necessary.

Officer Davis had to accelerate in order to make it through a berm that bordered the driveway. Davis found herself fishtailing as she fought to correct the cruiser. "Hold on, hold on, damn it." She looked up at the rearview mirror and smiled once the cruiser straightened out. "Sorry about that, guys." Maria changed her startled look into a pleasant smile as she nodded her head. Ricardo was busy watching out the side and glanced over his shoulder in time to see the Magic Trucking crew come busting through the berm — snow from the berm going all directions. Both vehicles drove down the rest of the driveway closer together. The further they drove, the easier it was to steer. The newly plowed driveway ran for another 50 yards through snowy high-walled berms on either side. A giant row of evergreens fought the snowy onslaught with branches batting at the snow.

Eventually, the trees revealed a man standing and waving a flashlight at the very end of the row. Chet assumed the man, standing in front of a big red barn, to be Mr. Olsen. Officer Davis confirmed his assumption, passing along Ricardo's message. The entire courtyard they drove into was somewhat shielded from the gusting winds, which was a relief to the travelers.

Mr. Olsen waved the two vehicles close to the barn doors and away from the howling wind. He did his best to direct traffic and couldn't believe anyone would be out driving in such a storm. As they passed, Mr. Olsen came up to the cruiser. Officer Davis couldn't roll down the passenger side window for Ricardo, it had frozen shut. Instead, Ricardo opened the door and reached out for a welcoming handshake.

"Ricardo. Good to see you young man. Georgia is so excited." Officer Davis smiled at Maria and grabbed her hand. It looked as though the man was choking up as he and Ricardo embraced. After a few seconds, Olsen continued. "We'd hoped… to see you again." He stuffed the flashlight back into his coat as he stepped back and pointed to where he wanted the two vehicles to park under a large wooden overhang with a metal roof attached to one side of the barn. The overhang would one day cover a motorhome the Olsen's hope to buy one day. For now, the Olsen's kept their tractor and other equipment in the covered area, but had moved them into the barn to make room for the visitors who journeyed their way. Both the cruiser and the truck managed to fit side by side, no problem.

The six travelers made their way toward the house as the snow fell and the wind continued to howl high above. As they did so, Mrs. Olsen came racing out of the house, nearly tripping as she ran in untied Sorel boots, black ski pants and matching jacket. The Olsens were in their mid 60's, but didn't look their ages, they looked much younger, lean and radiant.

Out of breath and spreading her arms wide, Georgia Olsen showed why she'd never met a stranger. "Well, hi everyone, welcome. We're so glad you found us, you had us both worried." When she set eyes on Ricardo she burst into tears. "Oh my God, Ricardo, come over here." The young man smiled and quickly ran to her. She gave him a motherly hug before pushing off, holding firmly onto his jacket, looking over his shoulder in order to get a better look at the young woman standing behind him. "Oh, this must be your Maria." Richardo nodded and introduced the pretty, dark haired, mother-to-be all wrapped up in a metallic warming blanket, who did her best to stand tall and smile.

Just as he began to introduce the others, Ricardo was interrupted when Maria started to moan, then *cry out*. Everyone froze. Mr. Olsen and Ricardo jumped into action and held onto Maria as Mrs. Olsen urged everyone to come quickly into the house. Ricardo was relieved when one of the biggest men he'd ever seen, offered to help. Seconds later, Goliath easily carried Maria up the deck steps as he followed the Olsen's inside.

"Welcome to our mess," Mrs. Olsen shouted as they entered the Olsen's farmhouse. The Olsen's were in the middle of remodeling their 1920's era ranch-style residence themselves. The kitchen and one bedroom had been completed, the rest of the house was cordoned off with floor to ceiling clear plastic. "Put her in the bedroom, prop her up, I'll get towels and warm water." Mrs. Olsen asked the Officer and Ricardo to stay and the rest to follow her husband.

Mr. Olsen gathered the four together in the kitchen. They stood around a butcher-block-topped island and welcomed the warmth from the wood fire coming from the brick fireplace at the opposite end of the kitchen. Mr. Olsen explained that they were all welcome to stay as long as necessary, but there was no room for all of them in the house — the barn would have to do. Their basement had been packed full of upstairs items, mostly paintings and furniture, the rest was in the barn. They had plenty of room to spread out in the huge barn. It would be a special time for them and the animals who'd already taken up residence.

§

Mellissa's eyes felt like they were on fire. Her hands were cold and her spirits were at an all time low. The thought that she may have hit bottom emotionally made her nervously chuckle to herself. Tears began to flow, causing that slight stinging sensation, once again, in her eyes.

She sat in her desk chair blinking, this time on purpose, bringing the one main wall monitor into focus. Mellissa had turned off two smaller wall monitors. There was no reason to keep them all running, she only needed one. Besides, she always liked to save on electricity. The monitor showed a dark image of the continuing flow of an upper atmospheric river, which meant there were no signs of the snow storm letting up any time soon. The dark image haunted her occasional day dreams that came involuntarily out of sheer exhaustion. The current storm front from the Cascades to eastern Washington had taken on the appearance of a dark green and black marbled abstract tongue that stuck out of a famous artist's painting in an attempt to intimidate the viewer. The apparition was coming after her, chasing her, she began to tremble as she grabbed both sides of her desk and held on as she looked down at her notes. She opened her stinging eyes and focused on the note pad where she had written her father's words of encouragement. "Stay strong, Mellissa." The journeyman weather forecaster felt helpless in that moment. The thought made her feel sick to her stomach.

Mellissa had been on duty for nearly 30, uninterrupted, hours and knew she needed to rest. The storm's intensity continued as the atmospheric river proved to be relentless.

The phone lines went down about an hour or two ago. Maybe longer, she couldn't remember. Until that happened people were asking for information she was hesitant to share. In a way, having the phones down was a blessing.

By now, all the Central Washington communities knew that they were in an extreme weather alert. Only people Mellissa recognized could reach her on her cell phone. She took a short break to walk outside after dressing for Arctic-like weather. She emptied the last of the five gallon can of fuel into the generator, which would give her 6–10 more hours of electricity depending on the electric load — *and then what?*

She slammed the station's heavy metal exterior door against the howling wind and leaned up against it for a few seconds. She was glad to be back inside. The refilling effort had become more difficult, which made her chuckle to herself. Mellissa felt more exhausted than when she ran the mile in high school for the first time. After hanging up her coat, she walked past her desk and entered Sonny's office, looking for the stash of sleeping bags and cots. There were times when the late night team would take turns napping on cots, provided by the government, during weather related emergencies like floods and forest fires, and sometimes snow storms. Last year there was a series of lightning strikes that needed to be monitored so Mellissa and Rod took turns napping overnight.

She found both in a storage closet and rolled out a sleeping bag on a cot in front of Sonny's desk. Mellissa set her phone alarm for 20 minutes, kicked off her shoes and climbed into the bag fully clothed. Just as she laid her head down on her rolled up coat, her phone rang. She knew it must be important and convinced her body to move. Mellissa looked at her phone — it was Rod.

"Mellissa? How are you holding up?" The sincerity in Rod's voice felt warm and encouraging. She hesitated, knowing she needed to be upbeat. She moved her head away from the phone and took a deep breath, then let it go.

Mellissa's last media update forecasted more snow, bringing the local total to just over four feet at the 1,000 foot elevation and eight to ten feet at 3,500 feet in the surrounding foothills. Mellissa's hesitation didn't go unnoticed by her friend. Rod could tell Mellissa was running on fumes and asked her to *just listen* — he had some good news. "My uncle is normally very busy, and was especially today, so he gave me a contact In Barrow, Alaska, the furthest weather service north. The person I spoke with happened to be on duty in a college weather monitoring room. I exchanged emails with her, an intern named Yura, who was able to concur with my calculations."

Rod's data showed that the atmospheric river flow had begun to diminish in size as it approached northern Alaska. There was silence on the other end of the phone. Rod waited for Mellissa's reply. "Mellissa?" He could hear her weeping, so he waited. After a few seconds, he heard the rustling of a chair moving across the floor and then a throat-clearing cough. "That's… good news, Rod, thanks for that. When…when do you and your uncle think we'll see some relief over the Cascades?" Rod knew Mellissa could figure that out for herself, but, most likely, didn't have the energy to put the calculations together. "By noon tomorrow in the Cascade region and in your area by two, three at the latest, that afternoon if the storm speed remains the same. But wait to release any update, Mellissa, until we see what the weather does when it reaches the Cascades."

Mellissa thanked Rod while looking down at the phone, both hands on her head, elbows on her thighs. She pushed the "off" button, made a note to send out a new release after checking the weather and a quick nap, reset her alarm, and crashed, face down, on the cot.

§

Pops Bellman wasn't the kind to sit and wait to hear from someone he cared about, especially his stranded weather-forecasting daughter. Mellissa had always made him proud and he couldn't imagine what she must be going through. Pop's cellphone call went to her voicemail. Frustrated, he left a quick message, asking for her to call when she could and hung up. He just wanted a damn phone call, a text, some form of contact. Even though Maggie shared his concern, she encouraged her husband to keep himself busy and try not to worry about their most independent thinking child. Maggie reminded Pops of the time a seven year-old Mellissa, along with two of her friends, made bracelets out of pipe cleaners and sold them door-to-door. "Her effort raised over $250 for the food bank that month," Maggie reminded Pops. Neither one of her parents thought Mellissa would raise a dime, let alone a few hundred dollars. "She'll be fine, Bruce, now go."

For the next two hours, Pops and a neighbor helped each other clear their respective driveways, for the second time that day, and pulled snow off of their respective patio covers. But the external distraction only helped for a while.

After Pops thanked his neighbor he put away the snow blower, hung up his shovel, and sat in the shed watching the snowfall while listening to the news on their battery-powered radio. When the weather update came on his thoughts went to a time when he would take Mellissa hunting with her older brother, Michael. Cindy and Chet were too young and Michael didn't mind that his younger sister tagged along. "Those two became very good at scouting and shooting," Pops shook his head thinking about how both of them were being challenged in life. The snow continued to fall and Pops made his way back into the house, pulling off his well-worn Sorel boots in the mud room, hanging his coat — heading for the warmth of their library and his easy chair.

Pops found it easy to brag about the accomplishments of each of his five children, he made no excuse for those conversations. And Mellissa seemed to be the one he favored most, because she never, ever, gave up. He couldn't stop thinking of her, now, as she sat at the weather station in the midst of the worst snowstorm anyone, even the national weather service, could remember for central Washington. In Mellissa's mind, her part of the world was under attack.

§

"Bruce, you're pacing again. Your worrying about Mellissa is going to wear out the carpet," Maggie had a comforting tone in her voice as she brought him a fresh cup of black coffee. "Thanks, Mag." Pops looked tired as he sat back in his big recliner. He took a sip and Maggie joined him with her tea in their cedar-lined library. Pops took another sip and carefully set the cup on one of the shelves he built the shelves he built years ago when they were first married. They both wanted a place where they could go and relax, while enjoying one of their favorite pastimes, reading. The room was modeled after a picture that Maggie had seen in a magazine devoted to farm life. Pops traded out his services for the lumber and constructed the room under Maggie's direction. It was one of the first of many projects they would work on together as they built their life together.

They loved to read, Maggie with her romantic mysteries and Pops favoring biographies of famous people — action/thrillers came in a close second. The shelves that lined three out of four walls were full from ceiling to baseboard on the specially built-in hickory shelves. Centered in the middle of the fourth wall stood a nineteenth century pot bellied stove that Maggie found in Odessa, south of Moses Lake, nearly 20 years ago. It was incumbent on Pops to keep the small relic going, especially when it's snowing and cold.

Normally, Pops and Maggie enjoyed their reading time together, but today was different. In addition to Mellissa's troubles, *The boys were out, risking their lives, God knows where, and here we sit praying for each of them.* Peter, the last time he called, told his parents that Chet and Michael weren't alone. It was somewhat reassuring that at least they're together in the truck with their big friend. Peter was home with his family and Cindy was safely home with Pops and Maggie, busy in the kitchen and checking in with the hospital's emergency service, online, monitoring their caseload. The ER would also be one of the first places Chet and Michael might show up if they were in trouble. In the meantime, Cindy chopped the veggies for the stir-fry she was preparing for dinner.

Chapter 14

"AND, BEHOLD, A CHILD IS BORN."

The governor of Washington State called in the National Guard to help with the record-breaking snow removal and the impact on other emergency services involving rescues of stranded travelers. Oregon and Idaho were close to doing the same if the storm continued to build across the Pacific Northwest. Alaska and western Canadian provinces of British Columbia and Alberta were experiencing unusual winter weather patterns, but nothing like Washington State, especially the central portion, which seemed to be hardest hit. The consensus of a Seattle-based meteorologist summed it up, "If Mother Nature was trying to make a point — she's succeeded."

The Olsen's were doing their best to accommodate the guests they expected and those they hadn't. The men were in the barn with Mr. Olsen, clearing out space for sleeping bags and setting up chairs to sit around visiting, while waiting for word about Maria and the baby. Mrs. Olsen prepared sandwiches and a big salad, while Davis stayed with Maria.

The men enjoyed the meal in the barn along with some lambs, two mules, two cows, and a big black labrador dog named Butch. The barn had one central light fixture in the center 30 feet above their heads. Two wall sconces helped to add light across from where the men sat.

The wind howled outside as if it wanted to disrupt the meal everyone enjoyed, especially Chet and Ricardo, who went for another sandwich. "Missy wants to know as soon as the baby is born, Ricardo." Ricardo nodded his head as he made his way from the sandwich tray to several bales of hay that had been hurriedly stacked to resemble a picnic bench. "My phone is back to 100% power, I'll call when…" his voice trailed off as Mr. Olsen's phone rang. " Yes, what? Great, wonderful, I will." He turned and looked at Ricardo, "It's a girl! I think you should go to the house now, son." The words no sooner left his mouth — Ricardo was off like a shot, slipping and plowing his way through two feet of fresh snow up to the back porch of the Olsen's home. Cheers of congratulations resounded through the barn as he left.

The guys continued congratulating among themselves when the smaller barn door opened. Officer Davis made her way in with the wind. She pushed the door shut with Sten's help, shook herself off, looked around the room and said, "Got any booze in here gentlemen?"

Sten smiled, held up a hand, and walked over to a beautiful walnut cabinet that looked a little out of place in the straw-lined barn. "I had to put my liquor cabinet out here while we are remodeling." He opened the top half by pulling two center handles apart and revealed a small bar backed by a mirror with bottles of various colors, mostly brown. He pulled the ice tray from the refrigerator standing close by and announced, "Whiskey, rum, and two choices of vodka, what's your pleasure officer?"

Michael, Goliath, and Chet watched as Mr. Olsen fixed the first drink, an old fashion, including the orange peel, for Officer Davis. He then took orders for everyone's favorite, plus beer for Chet. Officer Davis led the first toast, "Since my cruiser is now covered with snow, my captain said to remain in place, and since the highway is closed, let's celebrate Maria and Ricardo's new arrival, cheers to mom and the little one, boys!"

§

Local authorities in central Washington State welcomed the help from the Washington State National Guard troops and equipment. As a result, highways and major roadways began to emerge from under the deep white blanket that smothered everything as far as the eye could see. Roads became passable and traffic began to flow through deep-walled passageways. From above, the slow moving traffic looked like participants in a giant corn maze attempting to find the nearest exit.

Thanks to the addition of flags attached to car antennas or long poles and metal rods attached to vehicle bumpers to aid visibility over the plowed berms, accidents were kept to a minimum as pickup trucks and smaller vehicles could easily be seen at intersections where regular traffic signals flashed only their red lights indicating a four-way stop. Otherwise, drivers had to really watch for traffic as they emerged from under a horrendous blizzard in order to get back to normal.

The weather service sent out a news alert that forecasted a reduction in the 48-hour stormforce that had been confronting all municipalities from Anchorage to Vancouver, B. C., continuing down to Seattle and over the Cascade Mountains to central and onto eastern Washington State. The eight counties that comprised Central Washington State had been declared the hardest hit.

The average measurable snowfall had reached just over four feet in six out of the eight counties. Snowdrifts in the flat plains of Grant and surrounding counties where Moses Lake sat in the middle, had reached two to three times the reported average. Needless to say, the plow teams had their work cut out for them. It would take another day or two before any type of normalcy reached the main thoroughfares.

Mellissa sat with Sonny, who managed to reach the weather station by snowmobile. She had been on duty for nearly three days straight, mostly alone, monitoring the worst winter weather conditions ever to reach this part of the United States.

"Mellissa, we owe you a debt of gratitude for your service here at the station." She blushed slightly as Sonny went on to mention that a memo had been sent to the National Weather Service in Washington D.C., outlining the various weather forecasts that Mellissa had to make on her own. Her *Weather Alerts* were considered to be essential in saving lives throughout the communities the MLWS served. Not only that, but other stations keyed into the MLWS forecasts as the weather gained momentum. Neighboring stations watched as the storm traveled over the Cascades and onto the central and eastern portions of Washington State.

Both Sonny and Mellissa felt as though they were watching history in the making as they sat together monitoring the precedent setting weather pattern. Sonny had only been at the station for less than an hour and yet the place he'd basically built from the ground up looked and felt different. The normal buzz of anticipation from his employees that used to make him smile was gone. An unceasing howling wind replaced those thoughtful forecasting conversations as if declaring who was really in charge. But that's the way it's always been — the weather sets the pace and the forecasters do their best to anticipate what to expect. The only difference between the present and the past is that nature has the upper hand and it's wrapped around our throats — more threatening than predictable.

Sonny turned to Mellissa, who looked as though she didn't know if the sun was ever going to rise again, and made a suggestion. "Mellissa, call your parents, check in with them, and thank Pops for the use of his snowmobile."

§

Geraldo sat with his boss, in the Casa Grande or Grand House as Geraldo referred to it. Both men enjoyed their mutual favorite, 80 year-old-scotch from some remote island off the coast of Scotland. Geraldo carefully wiped his salt and pepper colored mustache after taking his first sip. Both men were silent in the moment. Jake watched his old friend sit back as a saxophone began to play from Jake's jazz collection. He wanted to make sure to say the right words. Normally, they'd be playing several hands of gin rummy and having a spirited conversation, but not now. Jake leaned back in his leather chair, closed his eyes, and thoughtfully asked Lillian for some help. After a few sips and a minute or two, Jake Hawthorne looked at one of the hardest working people he knew, smiled and said, "Congratulations my friend, or should I say, grandpa?" Geraldo leaned forward as both men raised a glass in unison. The moment they shared was emotional for both men as tears ran freely. "We need to toast again, my friend, this time to you," Geraldo said as he sat closer to Jake. "Thank you for all you do for my family, so, here's to you and the hopeful day you, sir, also become a grandfather. The two men shook hands after that toast and headed for the dining room where dinner was served.

Both men shared a deep respect for one another for different reasons. Even though both considered each other to be hard-working, their bond began to take shape years earlier when their children were young. It seemed like ages ago when both of their girls were playing together in the fields as the two men worked, from sunrise beyond sunset sometimes, digging post holes, stringing fence wire, and celebrating together as the small farm became a large working ranch.

Their work routine was carefully monitored by Jake's wife, Lillian. Together, Jake and Lillian spent a small inheritance of

Lillian's on 100 acres of land in a remote section of central Washington. They lived in a small shack that came with the land.

Geraldo was hired when he showed up on their doorstep with a small child, Maria, asking for work. The Hawthornes would look back on that day as a turning point in their lives, because of Geraldo's incredible work ethic and unlimited amount of knowledge when it came to farming.

Within two years their homestead had expanded its acreage to 500 and nearly 100 head of cattle. Horses, Lillian's favorite pastime, breeding and riding, came next. The ranch naturally expanded as did the Hawthorne family with the births of Tim and Missy. The development of the Hawthorne Ranch came faster than either Lillian or Jake could believe. By the time Tim was ready to graduate from high school, they had nearly 5,000 acres and a dozen people working under Geraldo's supervision. Maria and Missy became good friends, Maria, two years older than Maria, worked with Lillian on household duties, learning to cook and clean. Lillian treated Maria as one of her own and she and Missy became best friends.

Jake stood up out of the overstuffed leather arm chair and took a long stretch. "Waiting takes longer the older I get my friend." Geraldo agreed and suggested, "Add to that the thought of becoming 'un abuelo' — a grandfather and you're going to have to help me get up out of this chair." The two men slapped each other on the back as they headed to the billiard table for the necessary distraction of a game. Missy could be heard in the next room talking to Chet who called with the good news.

Jake walked over to the doorway and interrupted Missy, "Tell Chet that as soon as the roads are declared safe, we will drive north to pick up Ricardo, Maria and the baby." Geraldo smiled and nodded before lining up his shot.

§

Finally, it happened. The storm clouds that used to be dark and heavily ladened with ocean water, turned a lighter shade of gray, releasing the last vestiges of a snowy, less threatening delivery, into the Cascade Mountains. The angry atmospheric rivers that pummeled central Washington gradually disappeared. Further north, Alaskans living along the Bering Sea saw sunshine for the first time in a month. People living in the area were used to living in darkness for months at a time, but not this early in the season. The weather station in Utqiagvik where Yura works celebrated the changing weather pattern with big cheers as they sent out a sunny forecast — unusual for this time of year.

The wind that constructed large berms of snow throughout the central basin, including the community of Moses Lake, challenged travelers for days and sent semi trucks to the side of arterials and highways, including interstate 90. It caused major damage to buildings and homes and toppled thirty to sixty foot pine, birch, and poplar trees. That brutal force of wind suddenly became a slight breeze. The surprising shift in weather was nearly as alarming as it was welcoming.

Mellissa, fully rested and nourished with both of Bridgett's raspberry scones she'd left in the station's fridge, noticed the pattern along with Sonny, but barely had time to report it — it happened so fast. "It's always satisfying to send out good weather news, even if it's after the fact, Mellissa," Sonny said as he came from his office with a big sheet. A smile formed on Mellissa's face. Sonny added, "Keep sending out updates — make sure everyone knows this new weather pattern isn't going away or a fluke. Some people must be in shock over what has happened — praying and hoping for…for days." *How many days?* Mellissa thought to herself. Three or four? She couldn't remember. All she knew was that the worst had passed — just in time for Christmas.

Snowplows could be heard scraping the roadways and thoroughfares all over the region. Large plumes of snow were flying off other service areas from airports, railroads and mountain passes to parking lots and driveways. As the clouds began to lighten up the snow gave way to rays of sunshine. The temperature hovered around 30 degrees, but no one complained as long as the roads were passable, power was in the process of being restored, and loved ones were safe. Entire communities would remember this Christmas for many years to come.

§

Mrs. Olsen slept on a cot next to the baby's bassinet and Maria's bed. The baby would be waking soon in the antique bassinet, an Olsen family heirloom handed down from Sweden that dated back to the 18th century. Maria worked up the energy to raise her head. "You look tired, Maria, I have some oatmeal, blueberries and yogurt ready for breakfast." Mrs. Olsen put a second pillow behind Maria's head as the new mother pushed her way up into a sitting position. "You are so kind, Mrs. Olsen." "Please, call me Georgia." Maria clasped her hands together across her stomach, smiled and whispered, "Georgia, oatmeal with some blueberries sounds wonderful, I don't remember ever being this hungry."

Looking around the room, Maria added, "Where is everyone? Ricardo?" Mrs. Olsen had left the room, but returned quickly with a serving tray in her hands. "Everyone stayed in the barn last night. There's more room out there. Besides, I believe they celebrated the birth of your beautiful daughter…ah… Maria? The young mother glanced up in time to see Georgia

Olsen staring out the window. Maria turned her head but the glare of the sun hurt her eyes. "It's so bright out," Maria had to shade her eyes. But that wasn't what caught Georgia's attention. Chet, Michael, and Goliath were posing beside the Magic Trucking Company delivery truck after helping Sten clear that part of the driveway. Officer Davis appeared to be directing the shot as Sten Olsen leveled his phone to take a picture. "They look very happy to see the sun out," Maria replied as she readjusted herself in bed. "Look again, Maria, you won't believe it." Maria noted a sense of surprise in Georgia's voice as she looked out the window again. "Look at the side of the truck, Maria." What Maria saw made her cover her mouth. Outside in the very snowy Olsen courtyard stood three men in front of a truck that read: Magi Trucking. Georgia turned to Maria and in a slow deliberate tone, trying not to wake the baby as Maria kept eating, said, "We have a…a Christmas story here, Maria." Georgia then laid out the details of three men coming from the east, searching for a couple, the young mother with child, trying to find a place of refuge. "Those men, Chet, Michael, and Goliath, they are the Magi, Maria."

Before Maria could respond, Georgia was on the phone to a friend of hers who worked at the *Wenatchee Herald* newspaper. The reporter happened to be responsible for the editorial regarding Mother Nature's snowy onslaught a few days earlier. She had written a "Feel Good" story on the Olsen's when they moved into the area after leaving their jobs and starting over on the farm.

"Yes, three guys, I mean men, yes, three men who were brave and wise enough to find what they were looking for, baby's birth, young couple — it's a great story! Georgia's excitement for the story was shared by the rest of the group when they found out. Sten's photos were later sent to the paper and the rest was in the reporter's hands. The reporter did promise to try and get the story in by deadline in time for the Christmas Day edition.

When do you want to name the baby, or have you picked a name?" Maria had the look of a serene Madonna as her facial expression nearly spoke for her. "Yes, this little one will be named after both of our grandmothers, Isabella Rose." Georgia stopped and waited before setting the lunch tray down in front of Maria as the young mother shifted her weight in bed once again. Maria explained that her grandmother's first name is Isabella and Ricardo's, Rose. Both were still alive and living in Mexico. "That's such a beautiful name, Maria. Oh, and look, Isabella Rose, is beginning to stir." Georgia suggested Maria finish eating while she changed the baby. "I'll call Sten, when you finish lunch. We need to send a photo of the three of you to send to the *Wenatchee Herald*. The reporter made the request just now in a text. Looks like the story is happening! For now, though, let's just relax with Isabella Rose."

An hour later the men with help from Officer Davis completed plowing and shovelling out the truck, cruiser, and the driveway — all the way to the entrance to the highway. News of the storm letting up soon came over Officer Davis's radio earlier. Goliath ran the John Deere tractor with the plow attachment while the others hand shoveled. When the work outside was done, Ricardo excused himself and went directly to the house to be with Maria and Isabella Rose.

Chet let everyone know that Missy's father and Isabella's grandfather were on their way to pick up Maria, Ricardo and Isabella Rose. "They should be here in an hour or two if the roads are clear."

Chapter 15

Missy hurried to prepare for the arrival of Maria and the baby after talking with Georgia Olsen on the phone. Missy's father and Geraldo were on their way back to the ranch with Maria, Ricardo and little Isabella Rose. Jake drove the black Ford Expedition. Geraldo sat in the front passenger seat, watching and commenting on every move Isabella made during their drive back to the ranch. Maria and Ricardo held onto a custom made infant car seat that Sten and Michael fashioned together under Officer Davis's watchful eyes. "Just make sure the baby can't fly out of there if Jake has to stop fast, okay?" Isabella slept the whole way, riding safely in the middle back seat with her parents.

The Ford Expedition was second out of the Olsen's driveway. Chet, Michael, and Goliath followed in the Magi truck with Officer Davis leading the way, emergency lights on as they entered the newly plowed highway.

Missy was on pins and needles. Waiting patiently never suited her. She sat at the kitchen island going over a list she had revised several times, mostly because a baby would be joining them for Christmas.

The current plan included Maria and the baby staying in one of the guest rooms of the main house until further arrangements could be made. Missy could hardly believe that her childhood friend was now a *mother*. Tears slowly appeared as she realized how much life changed in the last 24 hours for the Hawthorne family, which also included Maria, Ricardo, the baby and, of course, dear Geraldo. Missy closed her laptop and walked over to the painting of her mother that hung in the living room. Her thoughts came clearly into focus as she smiled up at her mother standing proudly on a nearby hillside overlooking the ranch. She silently let her mother know that she would remain strong for her family — *I promise.*

Missy went from the living room to looking out the front window at the light snowfall. *Finally.* She had one more task to complete before everyone arrived. Without skipping a beat, she took the stairs two at a time heading for the guest bedroom. She stopped as she entered and took a deep breath, letting it out slowly Missy rolled the new comforter up the queen-sized bed. Fluffed the pillows one last time, turned on both side lamps, and exited, confident Maria's room was ready.

The guest room she prepared was located on the second floor, next to Tim's. There were four bedrooms in all, with the other two on the main level, in the 12,000 square foot log home with vaulted ceilings. Before leaving the Olsen's farm, Maria asked about sleeping arrangements, specifically a bed, for the baby, Georgia said not to worry.

After everyone left, Georgia called Missy Hawthorne. Maria gave Georgia the cell phone number of Missy Hawthorne's as Georgia requested. Missy didn't know the caller, but decided to take the call anyway. After introductions, Georgia explained that the guys were hauling a bassinet and some other essentials that the Olsen's were gifting their Ricardo and his new family. Georgia also mentioned the *Magi* incident in passing and the fact that the *Wenatchee World* expressed interest in doing a story. Missy and Georgia shared an emotional conversation that ended with Missy promising to call and confirm when the Magi caravan arrived. Although they had never met, both looked forward to meeting soon, and getting to know one another better. "We are so thankful that you and your husband were there for them."

§

The road to the weather station in Moses Lake was one of the first to be plowed. Sonny made a call to the city road crew boss, an old friend, with an emergency request. "We need to get the hell out of here, Ben." An hour later a road grader came slowly making its way up and then back down the long drive. The grader driver spent 30 minutes helping Sonny shovel out the parking area, enough to unveil both Mellissa and Sonny's cars. Moments after they finished, Mellissa said goodbye and Merry Christmas to Sonny and two weather forecasters entering the station.

Her Toyota 4Runner started right up, thankfully. Her trusty ride was a graduation gift from her parents and had been in the family for nearly 20 years. There was only one place she wanted to go as she slowly made her way down the newly plowed gravel drive, heading in that direction.

The Bellmans were just sitting down to dinner with Cindy when the doorbell rang. "I'll get it," Cindy said as she left the table. She returned arm-in-arm with her sister who looked as though she'd just completed a marathon run. Dark circles around Mellissa's eyes spoke volumes as her father stood, nearly dropping his napkin in his soup. Pops made it around the table in record time to embrace his weather-forecasting heroine. Maggie waited for her turn and dinner was delayed while Mellissa took a shower. As she walked off with Cindy by her side, Mellissa turned and laughingly declared, "I'll be right back. I've never been so hungry."

§

Enrique Valesquez Mara sat on the concrete floor in the holding pen of the Yakima County jail. Since returning from the emergency room for stitches and a few bandages, he'd turned in his street clothes for an orange jumpsuit with YC Jail on his back . He was awaiting a hearing and a meeting with a court appointed defense attorney. Things around the jail were happening in slow motion because his capture took place during Christmas week and the immense snowfall cleanup. Enrique had no idea what to expect, but one thing for sure, his future of living in America would, most likely, be put on hold.

Enrique's fellow pen mates, two men he guessed to be in their 30's, sat apart from each other awaiting their fate in the large concrete box of a room with no window and one wall of steel bars. The only conversation that could be heard came from a guard who was talking on his cell phone around the corner. The guard sounded upset to be working, but pleased to be making overtime pay. The thought of Christmas made Enrique smile as he looked up to see one of the men across from him looking straight at him. Enrique immediately looked down at the floor. Enrique didn't look back up, but he did respond, "Christmas, I'm sorry to be here at Christmas."

Enrique heard footsteps coming his way and glanced up in time to see the man sit next to him. When Enrique attempted to get up, the man pushed him back down. "So, you're sad to be here at Christmas time? Well, here's something to cheer you up." The man followed his response with three mighty blows to Enrique's head that rendered him unconscious. "There you go, Señor. No worries now, and you're welcome."

Unbeknownst to Enrique, travel plans were being made on his behalf. There would be no hearing or meeting with a defense attorney, there wasn't time. Two officers from Homeland Security's immigration deportation squad known as ICE came calling. They'd been tracking Enrique and his gang for months. Arrangements were made, paperwork signed off, and Enrique Valesquez Mara was on his way back to Mexico.

§

Peter worked the front-end loader dumping snow over to one side of the Receiving Area at Magic Trucking Company when Chet drove through the gate. Goliath and Michael were more than happy to end their truck delivery/rescue time with Chet. "Can't say it hasn't been fun, Chet." Michael said as he watched his step. Michael managed to make his way across the newly plowed surface without problem. Peter jumped down from the loader and joined the guys as they headed for the MTC office. "Well if it isn't the three wisemen coming in from the west this time." Peter took a selfie with his brothers and their friend in front of the "Magi" truck and posted it on his Facebook page.

The heat was turned up in the MTC office as the four gathered around the reception desk. Peter came in last, kicked off the snow and announced that he was the only one working snow removal since the snow had completely stopped falling. "I have three guys coming in an hour to do the rest and to make some last minute deliveries now that the roads are mostly clear in town." Chet and Michael offered to help with the clean up, but Peter insisted that they take off and get some well-deserved rest. "Besides, rumor has it that there's a big holiday dinner being planned between the Bellmans and the Hawthornes — you'll need your rest." Peter didn't have any more information, but told the guys to be prepared to get a call from Cindy or Missy later in the day with more details. All three nodded and smiled.

Goliath needed a ride to his office. "I have to find out what's going on. Mike, can you give me a lift?" Being asked to give someone a ride was a question he looked forward to since receiving his new leg.

Chet sat at one of the office desks and called Missy. He wanted to know more about the dinner Peter mentioned, but more importantly, how the new family was doing. Missy answered in a whispering voice, "Hey, Chet. I'm with Maria. She and the baby are asleep." Missy left the bedroom. Chet could hear her close the door, then a big sigh. "Ah, man, what a day! How's my delivery guy?" The two hadn't had any time together when the caravan arrived at the Hawthorne Ranch earlier. Chet could tell that Missy was tired and didn't bother to ask about the holiday dinner. Instead, he let Missy go knowing she'd be in touch.

The Magi crew made sure Maria, Isabella Rose and Ricardo's freight was delivered as safe and sound as the little family. Besides the vintage bassinet, several boxes of accessories for the baby, clothing, towels, bedding, linens were sent by the Olsens. Georgia Olsen wasn't sure why she'd kept them for so long — until Ricardo's return.

Missy greeted everyone and had everything ready for the new arrivals. Jake made sure the way was clear for Geraldo as the new grandfather carried his granddaughter up the front steps of the ranch house and down the hall to the guest bedroom. Maria, Ricardo and Missy followed close behind with Missy holding tightly to her dear friend. The bassinet and other items were warming in the living room while Missy and Maria changed the baby — a first for Missy. "Wow, hard to believe someone that small could poop that much." Missy's comment made them both laugh, which felt so good they both laid back on the bedspread with Isabella Rose in between wrapped in pink and lavender with a pink knit cap. "She's beautiful, Maria." Maria could hardly take her eyes off her baby as she responded, "Most importantly, she's safe, we're all safe."

§

The women: Missy, Cindy, Maggie, and Georgia were in charge of all arrangements for a holiday dinner that no one could have foreseen. When Missy asked her father for permission to host the dinner, Jake thought they had come up with a wonderful idea and fully supported it. Each family would celebrate Christmas Day at home, but on December 30th, 18 people total — five from the Hawthornes, including Jake, Geraldo, Maria, Ricardo, and Isabella. Nine from the Bellman family: Pops, Maggie, Mellissa, Cindy, Michael, Peter, his son and wife, Chet accepted the invitation, along with the Olsens. Goliath and Officer Davis were also coming. The ball was rolling and there was no stopping it.

Maggie and Georgia would be the chief cooks, Missy and Maria were in charge of decorations, Chet and Ricardo would be doing the shopping for food under strict instructions. Chet assured Missy he and Ricardo could handle the task. Georgia and Sten were bringing canned peaches for pie and pickles for the hors d'oeuvre tray. Geraldo and two men from the Magic Trucking Company would be busy removing snow on the Hawthorne property and part of the highway if necessary. Jake Hawthorne called Pops Bellman and renewed their old acquaintance. They had been involved in several central Washington community projects together years earlier. Pops enjoyed the call and told Jake he looked forward to sharing the holiday at the ranch.

After Georgia's call, Maggie told Pops that she could swear that they had stopped at the Olsen farm a couple of years ago and bought some produce. Maggie also offered to have Mellissa help out in the kitchen. "She's got the next two weeks off and wants to help out."

A record-breaking white Christmas Day finally arrived in the Pacific Northwest. A record amount of snow had been recorded by the 25th of December in Washington State —

and winter had just begun. In most cities across America, record amounts of anything weather related create headlines, as they did at the Wenatchee World newspaper. But another story deserved equal attention. The front page headline of the Christmas Day edition read:

Nativity Comes to Life in Wenatchee Valley
A child is Born!

Georgia Olsen's reporter contact wrote the most heart-warming story about the search and rescue of Maria, Ricardo, and the birth of Isabella Rose. Besides Georgia, she managed to interview Chet, Michael, Goliath, Maria and Officer Davis for the article. The reporter wove biblical references in with accounts from the men being able to follow a mysterious light in the sky during the snowstorm when they lost track of the highway. Sten's photographs helped to set the tone with snowy shots, showing the 3 "Wise Men" in front of the "Magi" labeled truck, who came out of the east in search of the couple expecting their first child. Jake Hawthorne had several copies of the Wenatchee World's special Christmas edition to hand out for souvenirs as people began to arrive for dinner.

The weather had calmed, but remained cold. The days were getting longer according to the celestial calendar, but no one involved with the holiday dinner at the Hawthorne Ranch seemed to notice — they were too busy enjoying the magic of the holiday.

Merry Christmas Everyone!

Acknowledgments

I've really enjoyed creating this story. I've always wanted to write a Christmas Story with a series of plot twists and like "Magic" it happened thanks to some very professional and creative people. Here they are,

- One of the most intelligent and patient editors I've had the pleasure of working with, a good friend, Rick. When he's not editing, Rick is an avid outdoorsman. Biking, hiking and paddling his way through the beautiful Northwest and beyond.

- Krista and Charlotte with the Spokane Weather Service for their time in educating me on the fundamentals relating to weather forecasting. My time at the station revealed a whole new world of service that became so intriguing I encourage young people to consider meteorology as a career option. How many people can actually say they held a deflated weather balloon before it was sent skyward? I will always think of my time with the local national weather service station when I watch the news.

- Two extremely creative colleagues, Kevin for his fourth cover design — this time with a holiday

twist and Russ for his skillful layout and helpful
internal design suggestions.

- Cathy Pirello for her patience and professional
  photographic skills in my office on a busy day.

- My cousin, Dennis, who has worked feverishly
  on creating a climate change scenario that will
  incorporate the whole world in a much needed
  clean up and liveable maintenance program
  for our planet. For more information contact:
  dustyrhodes.dr@gmail.com.
  He will gladly share more about his universally
  praised project titled: WISE-UP.

And Washington State for being so evergreen, mountainous,
and beautiful. A writer's dream state that lies in the midst of the
Pacific Northwest. *JP Robideaux*

* 9 7 9 8 2 1 8 3 9 2 9 4 9 *